# BOSS DADDY

SHANNA HANDEL

Published by Stormy Night Publications and Design, LLC.
www.StormyNightPublications.com

Cover design by Korey Mae Johnson
www.koreymaejohnson.com

Images by Dreamstime/Julie Lubick and iStock/4x6

1st Print Edition. January 2019

ISBN-13: 9781794446847

FOR AUDIENCES 18+ ONLY

This book is intended for adults only. Spanking and other sexual activities represented in this book are fantasies only, intended for adults.

# CHAPTER ONE

Always the wedding planner, never the bride.

My goal in life was to give my brides the weddings of their dreams. Turn their stress into excitement. Stretch every dollar of their budget to its fullest potential and give them the day they had been dreaming of since they were a little girl.

They say, 'do what you know.' What I knew was how to throw a tear-jerking, smile-stretching, memory-yielding, one-of-a-kind wedding.

As a child, I'd learned to read flipping through the glossy pages of my favorite bridal magazines. For my birthdays I would ask for craft supplies. With little bits of tulle and strings of plastic pearls, I decorated my dollhouse with a romantic flair that even Barbie envied. My little sister Josie never tired of being marched down my makeshift aisles. Whether they were in the backyard, or down the hallway of our house, time and time again she would happily come to the altar at the end and marry her favorite teddy bear, Mr. Sparkles.

I'd watched every wedding movie my mother would allow me to. The only time I remember getting in trouble as a child was when I snuck out with a friend to the theater to see *Runaway Bride* when I was supposed to be studying for a math test.

I was obsessed.

It all started after my father abruptly left us. He had been an absentee father all along—worked long hours then came home and sat in front of the TV—but having him disappear altogether was devastating. I could still hear his tires crunching over the gravel as he pulled out of our driveway for the last time. My mom tried to hide her tears, but I knew she was lonely.

We never spoke of my dad.

My mom was a beautiful, generous, loving woman and she deserved to have a great guy. In my mind, one day she would meet the real love of her life, a man who would always care for her and never leave her. They would have a big, gorgeous ceremony to celebrate their union. Josie and I would dress up in pink satin dresses and hold Mom's bouquet for her while she and her groom—our new, loving father—exchanged vows.

It never happened.

By my freshman year of high school, it was obvious my mother was not interested in meeting anyone. I began to wonder why Mom and Dad had come together in the first place. One day after scouring our house for wedding albums, and finding none, I worked up the courage to ask her how she had met my father.

We sat at our four-seater kitchen table, the dim light hanging above us making the lines in her face show how much she aged over the past decade. Placing her hand over mine, her skin feathery soft, she told me. "It was a long time ago—gosh, I was just eighteen, maybe just turned nineteen? I did pageants back in those days—"

"You did? I had no idea," I said.

A sadness fell over her tired face. "I hid it from you girls. I didn't want to make it seem glamorous." Her tone turned cold as she said, "It wasn't."

"Okay, well, what happened?" I asked.

"I won the Bluebonnet Miss Teen crown. My small town of Texas went wild. They even threw me a parade." She gave a disgusted chuckle. "There wasn't much going on in that town. Having a local girl win such a big crown really gave them something to talk about. After that day I had men coming in and out of the ice cream parlor I worked at, just wanting to catch a glimpse of Miss Bluebonnet in person. Gosh, I sold a lot of double scoops that month."

She got quiet and I could sense we were getting to the part about her meeting my dad. Not wanting her to stop talking, I prodded her, "Is that how you met Dad? Was he one of the ones who came in to get a glimpse of you?"

Her eyes turned to me. A mixture of happy times washed away by sadness reflected at me. "No. Just the opposite. He was originally from Texas but now lived out of town... Wyoming to be exact. He was in there meeting with the local pharmacy—he sold the machines that count out the pills manually, so the pharmacist didn't have to. Anyway, he was... sweet, and polite. And so different from the other men who had come into the parlor—he had no idea I was a beauty queen. When he left, he asked if he could take me to dinner that night."

"And what did you say?" I was on the edge of my seat, hungry for a story of romance, of love.

"I said yes. I was flattered, I suppose. He was a little bit older than the other boyfriends I'd had. And he had a steady, grownup job; that meant something to me. And of course, as you know, he was handsome."

"Where did he take you?"

"He took me to a little Italian place. I felt so grown up. There was a white cloth on the table, candles, linen napkins, the whole nine yards. I was so nervous, I barely knew how to act—luckily the pageant had required me to take an etiquette course, so I made my way through the three courses just fine. Your father even snuck me my first glass of wine." A small smile spread across her face as she looked past me, her eyes focusing on nothing as her memories washed over her.

"Well, what happened after that? Did he kiss you when he took you home?" Her gaze came back to me. I couldn't read the look that rested in her eyes. "What is it, Mom?"

"Louanne, I went back to his hotel room with him."

"Oh. I... ah..."

Her hand squeezed mine. "And you were born nine months later."

My breath caught in my throat. I felt like a cold sweat was going to break out over my forehead. I was the only reason my parents were together? Just a one-night stand... an unplanned pregnancy? "Mom, I—"

"Louanne Dixon. I wouldn't have it any other way. Seeing your little face, the moment after you were born, honey, that was the most magical moment of my life. And the way you reached up and instantly wrapped your tiny little fingers around mine—it was like you already knew me. And then, he gave me Josie. You girls are the most precious thing in my life and I'd take all the pain your dad gave me in exchange for the joy of having you both," she said.

We cried then, buckets of tears, trying to stay quiet so we didn't wake Josie.

Instead of marrying, my mom got a nursing degree and spent her days working providing for my sister and me. I took care of Josie, and with no mom available to run me to soccer practices or dance recitals, I had a lot of time on my hands. I spent it developing my passion for creating all things wedding. And now, I got to live out my dream.

I stayed incredibly busy, especially in spring—that's what I call 'Wedding Season.' There are cakes to be ordered, menus to be prepared, staff to hire and train, and my favorite—decorations to be planned, purchased, and carefully laid out. Throw in music, a dance floor, and a few signature Louanne Dixon touches to 'wow' each unique bride, and you had yourself a wedding they would (hopefully) be talking about for years to come.

I gave each of my weddings a nickname that reflected its

theme. For example, one of my favorites I dubbed Wedding at the Castle. The bride was a princess at heart. For her, I found mock cut-crystal goblets and decanters at the dollar store. I placed translucent glass plates over silver chargers, and voilà! With only four dollars spent per head I had a dinner setting fit for royalty. Each place was set with a tiny, sparkling tiara for the female guests, and a gold crown for the men. (I had begged the manager at the Burger Barn to part with fifty of his cardboard kiddie crowns, then spray painted them gold.)

Thousands of lights were strung from the rafters above the dance floor. Not only did they give a romantic glow to the room—and add a touch of whimsy—the tiny lights performed a much more important task. As the bride twirled on the floor with her groom, the Swarovski crystals and beads that were embroidered on her ivory gown reflected the light, creating a dazzling, sparkling effect that made her look like a real live princess.

The bride and groom left the reception in a horse-drawn carriage.

Planning weddings was what I lived for. Seeing the bride's face absolutely light up the first time she walked into the barn for the ceremony made it worth every minute.

From time to time, a client would ask me, "Doesn't it get old? Always being the wedding planner, but never being the bride?" Did it get lonely at times? Sure. Was I fearful that I would become my mother, hiding my tears and crying myself to sleep in the dark night? Of course. But getting married myself just hadn't been on my mind. I had too much to do. And so, when people asked if I was lonely, I told them 'no.'

And that had been true. Until very recently.

Before *his* return, I was happy. My sister Josie had recently turned twenty-one and we would have a glass of wine together once a week. I took my mom shopping and out for manicures. And, I worked. But then, my lifelong crush came back to work on his family's ranch—the very ranch at which I was the event planner. And his presence made it difficult for me to put my nonexistent love life aside and focus solely on work.

Hayes was back and his very nearness made my skin feel all tingly. When he would lean over me to see my computer screen, his clean, masculine scent would waft my way. His arm would brush against mine and goosebumps would rise on my skin. Just hearing him say 'Louanne,' in that slightly southern accent he had brought back to the ranch with him made my panties damp.

*Hayes Jenkins.*

The all-American boy next door I had known since grade school.

I thought about the day he walked into our social studies class. Little Peak was a tiny town, kids bussed in from all around the rural area—some riding for over an hour to get to school. Everyone knew each other, their families all knew one another, so a new kid showing up was a huge deal.

Hayes had stood at the front of the classroom, looking confident beyond his years as the teacher introduced him.

"Class, this is Hayes Jenkins. He and his younger brother Colton are transferring to our school, from Jackson. His family bought the Turner ranch. His older brother, Brody Jenkins will be taking over the Turners' cattle ranch operation, as well as adding vacation cabins. They have renamed the ranch, CLAS. It stands for 'clean living and sunshine,' meaning there will be no drugs or alcohol tolerated on the property—you could all take a page from Brody's book, we will be discussing the dangers of those substances later this semester. The town is excited for the Jenkinses to bring some wholesome fun to the community. Please make the Jenkinses feel welcomed here in Little Peak."

Some of the kids had latched on to our teacher's admiration of what CLAS stood for and tried to tease Hayes about his brother Brody's 'clean living.' Hayes wouldn't have it and after a few playground scuffles, he had won the respect of the boys. He already had the whispered admiration of the girls.

Our mothers met at Little Peak Baptist church and became good friends. When my mother wasn't working, her, my sister and I were frequent visitors on the ranch. Hayes and I played tag, rode horses. When we were older, we hung out together, had the same friends. My junior year, his older brother and ranch owner, Brody, hired me as a part-time employee, helping out on the weekend. I was super organized and loved to make things pretty, so I was a no-brainer to be his assistant when he needed help with event planning.

When I graduated high school, Brody asked me to come work at CLAS for the summer. He was busy hosting corporate retreats, family reunions, that sort of thing, but wanted to take on weddings. The business was growing, and he needed help. I quickly obliged.

And never left.

After that summer, I chose a college close to home, returning every weekend to work. I'd stay with my mom in town or if an event had overnight guests (which we almost always did) I would stay in the women's bunkhouse on the ranch.

Hayes had the most serious disposition of the four Jenkins brothers. Anything he undertook he gave his all. College was no exception. After being offered a full academic scholarship to the University of North Carolina at Chapel Hill's business school, he waved goodbye and headed south. The program was intense. Hayes was offered internship after internship and we rarely saw him. After he graduated, he went on to get his MBA, while working full-time as a risk management analyst, ensuring that corporate policies adhere to governmental regulations—the perfect job for a serious guy. He came home for the occasional holiday and roundup days, but over the six years he was gone, we rarely saw one another.

While Hayes was busy slaying the business world in

North Carolina, I remained focused on my work in Wyoming. As the event side of things on the ranch continued to grow, so did my responsibilities. My junior year of college, I switched to all online courses and continued to work the ranch, living with my mom in town. I spent nights hunched over my computer, trying to ignore the gorgeous wedding décor on Pinterest and focus on my online classes. That was a busy two years and I had no time for a social life, much less my boyfriend at the time. I loved him, but I loved ranch life and my work more. He eventually dumped me.

I haven't dated since.

I graduated college with my own degree in business—though my GPA was a full point below Hayes'. On the day of my graduation, Brody gave me a triple chocolate cake (courtesy of Memaw) and a yearly salary plus benefits. I became the full-time event planner for CLAS ranch. I bought myself a cute little house in town. And I worked. The years went by in a pleasant, bustling manner. Georgia moved onto the ranch, she and Brody started dating and eventually married. The second eldest Jenkins brother, Travis, finished up his doctorate program and met and married Bridgette. They had the cutest little girl, Lila Bell.

Since the oldest two brothers had gotten married and the business continued to expand, Brody split the ranch up into co-owners. Brody oversaw business deals and finances. Travis, with his PhD in animal husbandry ran the cattle ranch. Brody's wife Georgia, a vet tech, became Travis' assistant. Colton, the youngest brother, was responsible for all things recreation—fishing, boating, day trips to Jackson Hole, horseback riding lessons. Keeping the weekend guests happy. Their grandmother, Memaw, oversaw the onsite restaurant, the Mess Hall. She chased her staff—which often consisted of her grandsons—around with her wooden spoon, bossing and cooking the best food in Wyoming.

Then, after six years of being gone, out of nowhere, with no real explanation, Hayes had returned to the ranch.

Brody cut him into the business. With Hayes' MBA, no-nonsense personality and perfect organizational skills—that were only second to my own—he was a perfect match to oversee events. I implemented the planning and carrying out of the parties while Hayes saw to all of the scheduling, budgeting, vendor relations, and repair and maintenance of the buildings we used. Recently, he was taking on developing relationships with small businesses in order to create a gift shop for visitors by selling products from local entrepreneurs.

Hayes managed one full-time employee. And that was me.

Though Hayes and I had never been more than friends, during our teen years there was the inevitable tug and pull of sexual tension running between us. Beyond a little harmless flirting, nothing ever came of it. The closest thing that had approached crossing that line of friendship had happened one night when Hayes was home for the holidays, the two of us laid in the bed of his truck after a long day of work on the ranch. The stars stretched over us like a dotted blanket. The full moon glowed so brightly, we could see one another's faces clearly. We laughed and chatted, attempting to name the constellations we saw. That night, Hayes had given me the nickname, Luna the moon goddess, because of how beautiful he thought I looked under the moonlight. I still remember how his compliment made my cheeks burn with shyness and pleasure. I thought he was going to kiss me that night, but he didn't. He still calls me Luna, and it makes me blush.

Now that we were both single, grown adults working together, I felt that same hormonal teen attraction. If he was walking by and accidently brushed against me, delicious shivers ran down my spine. Once in a while, we would disagree about something. His brow would rise sternly, and he would take 'that tone' with me—the one that made my pussy tingly and melty.

Hayes was back. Forever. And that's how my crush

became my boss.

But none of that mattered. I was a professional woman and I would not date my boss. Also, I was going to have to remind him who was in charge of events on the ranch. A few times we had gone head to head over safety concerns—him having the mind of a risk analysist. He had nixed the fire dancers I ordered for Luau under the Stars—too dangerous. Killed the gymnast hanging on silk threads from the false beams—'false beams mean false, Luna… they can't hold weight.' And most recently, he had asked me to stop using real candles—'total fire hazard, not worth the risk involved when there are perfectly good LED lights on the market these days.'

Can you imagine? Tacky battery-operated lights at one of *my* weddings? Please.

That was the final straw. I simply ignored his request and went on with my decorating. After all, I'm a professional, experienced wedding planner. And these brides would not have tears in their eyes over their big day without things going my way. I don't mean to sound rude, but I know what I'm doing, and Hayes needed to back up and let me do it.

He would just have to remember that even though he oversees the events department, I do the weddings—and what I say goes.

•  •  •  •  •  •  •

"Hayes Jenkins, you put that wooden spoon down, *right this instant!*" I narrowed my brows, throwing my hands on my hips for good measure. I hoped my tone sounded angry enough to hide the fear I felt inside. I trembled at the sight of the implement in the broad hand of the six-foot two-inch cowboy who stood before me.

A slow grin spread across Hayes' face, his white teeth sparkling at me from underneath his full lips. Running his free hand through his sandy hair, his blue-gray eyes focused on mine. The determination that flashed within his gaze sent a shiver down my spine as I inched away.

"I'll put this spoon down when I'm finished with it. And not a moment sooner." Like a predator stalking its prey, Hayes slid toward me. His long, lean muscles rippled underneath his shirt as he casually swung the spoon in his hand.

Feigning confidence, I expertly flipped my hair over my shoulder. "And what exactly do you mean to do with it, may I-I ask?" I stuttered, knowing full well what a Jenkins man used a wooden spoon for. My bottom bumped into the countertop behind me. My hands gripped the ledge. I was trapped, facing my stalker.

Hayes took another stride toward me. His left palm rose in the air, opening and lying flat before him. His right hand lifted the spoon, tapping his empty, outstretched palm with the smooth, round end. A light 'smack' filled the room each time it landed. "I think… Louanne… you of all people know exactly what I intend to do with this spoon. After all, you have worked on the ranch longer than any other employee. Flip that beautiful golden-brown hair at me all day—it doesn't change a thing."

My buttocks clenched beneath my skirt. I pressed my backside further into the counter behind me, as if to protect my asset. "Hayes Jenkins, I will say it one more time. You put that spoon down, *right now.*"

"Or what?" he asked, cockily raising a brow at me.

"Or, or… I'll scream!" I shouted.

He chuckled. "Go ahead. No one will hear you. And if they did, they all know better than to interrupt a man correcting his woman."

I gasped. "I am *not* your woman. I am your *employee* and you have no right to lay a finger on me. It's… it's… illegal! Not to mention distasteful—"

The grin dropped from his lips. "Let me tell you what I find distasteful, Louanne. Little girls that mouth off to their bosses with a disrespectful tone."

He had me there. Just moments ago we'd been in a

heated argument in front of the other staff. Okay—I had been in a heated argument. Hayes had just stood there, his jaw getting more and more tense with every nasty word I threw out, his blue eyes turning a stormy gray.

I had been shocked when he'd taken my upper arm in his firm grip and guided me to the kitchen off the Mess Hall, where I now found myself stuttering my way through my defense. "I-I was just telling you that you were doing everything... wrong. I have a certain way I do things. And that way is the right way. And when some big... brute comes in and messes everything up, then yes, I get angry."

He took a long-suffering breath. "The way you had the gauze set up around candles was a fire hazard. And as your boss, I am not going to watch this ranch burn down just to appease you. I know you've done things your way on the ranch for a long time. And bless my brother's soul—you seem to be the only woman in the world Brody lets have their way with everything. But I'm your boss for a reason. And that reason is that sometimes you require a little direction. Which I am more than happy to give to you. Now, would you like to apologize for that sassy tone you took with me? Or maybe for questioning my judgement? Disrespecting me in front of the staff?" He gave me a long stare.

I crossed my arms over my chest. I was still fuming. "Every good decorator knows that battery-powered LED lights are for people that don't have enough class to light a real candle. They are tacky, and I will have no part in it." I turned my nose up at him.

One brow lowered over his now steel gray eyes. His arms crossed over his chest—spoon still in hand—his forearms pushing up his bulging biceps until they looked enormous. When he spoke, his voice was laced with danger. "Are you saying you aren't going to work this wedding?"

"I'm saying that if there is anything in this wedding powered by a battery, then I'm not going to be there to witness it," I sniffed.

His chiseled jaw tightened. "Are you sure you want to give your boss an ultimatum, Luna?"

How dare he use his special nickname for me at time like this! Luna, my foot. I took a deep breath, steadying my nerves and steeling my trembling voice. "I'm saying I do things my way, or not at all."

His eyes narrowed at me, his head shaking in frustration. "And *that*, little missy, is exactly why I am holding this spoon. You are one little girl that is in dire need of a severe attitude adjustment. Brody has gone on too long letting you have your way at every turn. I'm your boss now and boss you I must. And it starts with a good old-fashioned spanking, young lady."

My heart stopped beating in my chest. My jaw dropped wide open. A white-hot heat spread across my face. A ball of ice formed in my stomach.

"You wouldn't dare," I whispered, knowing full well he would.

"Being back the past few weeks made me realize I was the only one who *would* dare," he said.

"Dare to what?" I gasped.

He said, "Put you in your place, Louanne. Take control of your out of control, over-controlling manner. There is no doubt you excel at your job and you bring in a healthy income for the ranch. But the way you do it—it's abrasive. It's been your way or the highway for too long around here. And that changes, now."

I threw my hands in the air, protesting, "But the way I run things is how I get the job done! Brody says that my personal style is the reason the event side of the ranch is making so much money. We have people coming from all over the country to experience my country chic weddings. Not to brag but—"

"You are bragging. And the one thing you seem to be forgetting is that the only way you got to where you are is with the assistance of other members of this team answering each and every beck and call of yours and never questioning a single one of your decisions. It stops now. The only way to help you see your bratty behavior is by treating you as any cowboy gentleman would when a brat comes along his path—redden her bottom and spank the sass right out of her," he said.

Was he being serious? I answered my own question with another question—was Hayes ever not serious? He was really going to spank me! Right here in the kitchen where anyone in the Mess Hall could hear.

My hands went to my bottom, grabbing it as if I could protect it. My eyes slid to the exit that was just to Hayes' left. I wasn't the high school track team sprint champ for nothing—I could make it... if I just slid past him and made a break for it, I could outrun him. Sure, he had his brute strength. But I was slight and quick. Sophomore year there wasn't a boy at Little Peak High that could out run me.

Taking a big gulp of air, I look up at Hayes from underneath my mascaraed lashes, feigning sincerity. "Hayes, you're right. I've been... a bit... extra. What do you say we—" looking toward the exit, I brought my arms up by my sides and lunged past him, flinging myself toward the bright red 'exit' sign, calling over my shoulder as I fled, "—finish this conversation some other time!"

Adrenaline rushed through my veins, my heart thumping against my ribs as I made my escape. A smile started to stretch its way across my face as I neared the door. I was going to make it!

"Oomphf!" A sharp tug on the waist of my skirt made me momentarily lurch forward, then, like when you hit the brakes too hard in your car, I was pulled back, straight into the rock-hard arms of Hayes. My back pressed against his chest, his arms locked around me. If I wasn't so terrified of what was to come—and panting to catch my breath—I might have relaxed into his arms. The hold felt... nice. His body heat wrapped around me like a blanket. My shoulder blades pressed against his strong muscles.

He whispered in my ear, "That was cute. Reminded me

of watching you run the high school track in those tiny little burgundy shorts, years ago. Where did you think you were going exactly?"

Clearing my throat, I focused on getting myself out of trouble. If I couldn't avoid this punishment by running, maybe I could talk my way out of it. I squeaked, "I-I'm sorry, Hayes. You're right. It won't happen again, I promise." Strong hands moved to my shoulders. Slowly, he turned me to face him. His gaze was only inches from me.

"It most certainly will happen again, Louanne. I'm sure of it. And when it does, I will do then, what I am going to do now. Spank your ass." With that, he grabbed hold of my hand with one of his, and with his other hand, snatched the abandoned spoon from the top of the big kitchen island. Before I had time to protest, Hayes had me bent over the island. My stomach dug into the ledge as my chest pressed against the cool metal of the stainless-steel top. The hand he held was suddenly wrenched behind me and attached to my lower back. My free hand pressed into the island, steadying my upper half.

This was really happening. After all the years of working with Jenkins men—men who were notorious for running a tight ship and disciplining sassy woman—I was going to be spanked by one. And spanked by not just any one of the four drop dead gorgeous muscle-laden brothers—it would be the one I had practically had a lifelong crush on.

Hayes.

My mouth was dry, my tongue like sandpaper. I had no words. My body tightened into one frozen Louanne Popsicle. The ice that was forming in my stomach grew into baseball-size hail. Funnily enough in my arctic state, underneath my skirt, my pussy was a hot, melty mess.

My cheeks burned as Hayes tightened his grip on the hand he held behind my back. His other hand went to the hem of my skirt.

"Hayes, no! Please... don't!" I protested as the material went up and over my waist. Cool air rushed over my panty-clad bottom. Goosebumps rose up and down the backs of my bare thighs. I squeezed my eyes shut tight. This was not happening.

Then, the first whack of the wooden spoon landed on my panty-covered rear end. "Ouch!" I cried. A burning sensation immediately danced over my skin, the heat growing as it traveled. "That hurt!"

"Spankings hurt," he said.

*No shit, Sherlock,* I screamed in my mind. I could sense him raising the spoon again. My face tightened, my buttocks clenched as I braced for the impact. This spank landed on the curve of my bottom—not protected by my thin undergarments. The sting was twice as bad on bare skin. I sucked air in between my teeth. I hissed under my breath, "Mother Mary!"

"Oh, Louanne, we are just getting started," he chuckled.

"What?" I gasped. The two smacks of the spoon were the most physical discipline I had ever received in my life—and I had had enough. "Please, Hayes. I'll be good. I promise! What do you want me to do? I'll do it! I'll apologize in front of the—damn it, Hayes, that hurt!" The fire spread as the spoon came down two more times in quick succession. The spanks were getting harder. I could feel my bottom jiggling under the wooden implement. The fiery pain spread. I danced from tiptoe to tiptoe. I longed to rub the sting out with the hand he held behind my back.

"Am I getting through to you? Do you understand where an attitude gets you?" he asked.

"Bent over an island having my rear end beat like a meringue?" I cried.

"Ah. Still sassy, I see. The spoon isn't working for you. Let's get these panties down and I'll handle that beautiful bare ass with my hand," he said.

This could not happen. The man I had known all my life and who had recently become my boss could not see my bare bottom, much less spank it like a daddy spanking his little girl. "Hayes, let's talk this through—"

"The time for talking is over," he said. His fingertips hooked into the elastic waist of my cotton panties. I could feel them being pulled down as my bottom was slowly exposed to him. My cheeks burned furiously—though not as bad as the lower set of cheeks currently were. Again, I squeezed my eyes shut tight as if to block out the humiliation of what was happening.

Hayes continued to lower my panties until they were just under the curve of my bottom, resting around the tops of my thighs. "Now I'm going to spank your bare bottom with my hand until you are one very sorry little girl."

"But I am sorry!" I protested. I tried to peek at him over my shoulder, showing him my earnest face. Surely he would see how remorseful I was and pull those panties right back up into place! No such luck. All I got was a glimpse of his clenched jaw and the determination flashing in his eyes. His huge, paddle-like hand rose in the air.

His hand came down on my bare skin. A warm, tingly sensation spread over my bottom. Shockingly, it was a pleasurable sort of pain that danced over my jiggling ass cheek. To my surprise, my pussy clenched, leaking juices of excitement. Hayes' husky voice demanded, "Spread your legs a little further."

But I was a good girl. And good girls didn't do that sort of thing. My mind pictured myself from an aerial view. If I were to spread my legs, what would he be able to see? My wondering ended quickly as a sharp, stinging swat landed on the center of my left cheek.

"That's going to leave a mark," I hissed between my teeth. It was a warning smack—I had no doubt—and left me aching for the sexier, lighter spank he had first given me with his bare hand. Gulping, I obeyed his demands. Inching my feet apart, I spread my legs against the constraint of the elastic panty band around my thighs. The cool air now rose between the cheeks of my ass, traveling up my cleft. And no doubt making the shiny wetness of my arousal visible to Hayes. To my intense shame, I could smell the musky scent of my wet pussy filling the air.

Could Hayes? Did he know how much this punishment was turning me on? Did he know that for years I had been curious what it would be like to be taken in hand by him? The questions left my mind as his hand began coming down in earnest. I was getting the spanking I had earned by mouthing off to my boss in the Mess Hall. Sexy feelings melted into panic as my ass was lit up by the fiery spanks. I was shocked by how quickly the pleasure turned to pain. And how much it was making my pussy pulse to have him control me like this.

His fingers tightened around my wrist. When he spoke, his firm tone made my pussy quiver. "As your boss I will now oversee your ass as well as your work. If your attitude is snappy, sassy, too bossy, your bottom is going to pay."

"Isn't that something I should have to agree to?" I asked between clenched teeth, tears springing in the backs of my eyes at the pain.

"You already did." His hand landed twice more in the same exact spot.

"How so?" I asked, dancing on my tiptoes and trying to keep the sass, and the tears, from my voice.

"By coming into the kitchen with me. You knew that you had earned a spanking. You knew that I was going to give you one. And you wanted it," he stated.

"You dragged me in here by my arm! I tried to run away the second you made your intentions clear!" I protested.

His hand paused in the air. "So, you are telling me, you've never wondered what it would be like to be spanked by a Jenkins man?"

"Err… that's not what we're talking about. You were saying I agreed to being spanked—which I did not. Wondering… that's different." The pause in the spanking gave me a moment to catch my breath. But now, the stinging was turning to a pulsing, throbbing feeling. How I longed to rub my poor bottom!

"But you did come with me. And you don't deny you

deserved a spanking, do you?" he asked.

I had been over the top defiant with him earlier. But admit I needed a spanking? Never. "Um... does a grown woman ever need a spanking?" I squeaked.

"In my humble opinion, almost every day. Especially a woman like you," he said.

My bottom ached. What could I do to end this? I didn't think I would be able to make it much longer without crying. He had already seen my bare bottom—he didn't need to see me cry, too. "I'm really sorry. You were right about the candles. And I shouldn't have sassed you like that—especially in front of the staff. I-I've learned my lesson and I'd like to get back to work. Are you... finished?"

"You tell me. I think you need a few more spanks." His mouth moved to my ear, his hot whispered words tickled my earlobe, melting my core. "I think you need a daddy to tell you you're a naughty girl. Bend you over his knee and properly spank your bare bottom till you are crying and begging to be let up. What do you think?"

Heat crawled up my neck, flooding my face. More moisture pooled between my legs as my knees turned to jelly. "I- I... uh..."

"That's what I thought," he said. I could hear the grin in his voice.

My panties were put in place. My skirt neatly situated back over my burning bottom. Hayes released my hand, pulling me gently to an upright position.

I fought through my freshly spanked shame and forced my gaze to meet his. Our eyes locked. My heart fluttered at what I could sense within his eyes.

Things between us had shifted.

Despite my punished bottom and utter humiliation at my sexual response to Hayes correction, I smiled up at him.

Smiling back, he gathered me into his arms. "There's a good girl."

• • • • • • •

Weeks went by, a thin band of tension running between Hayes and me. To my surprise, the spanking had changed my attitude. I hadn't realized that I had fallen into a habit of barking commands to my colleagues and snipping at them if things weren't done perfectly to my liking. The memory of Hayes pulling down my panties and baring my bottom forced me to bite my tongue on more than one occasion.

But the spanking had done more than tame my words. It showed me my feeling for Hayes had grown to more than a crush. He'd been back on the ranch for a few months now, and I had to admit the best part of my day was whenever he walked into a room.

Our relationship remained professional, if not a tad more flirty than usual after the spanking. But things had been so busy on the ranch—it was spring, wedding season—I didn't have much time to process my feelings.

Brody was taking the staff out to dinner to celebrate a job well done and give us a much-needed break after five event weekends in a row. He had recently discovered a little Italian place that had just opened one town over and wanted to treat the crew. We all piled up into the CLAS ranch minibus—the sides proudly proclaiming in blue paint, *Clean Living And Sunshine*. Hayes squeezed into the empty seat next to me at the last moment. The heat from his arm as it brushed against mine sent electric tingles over my skin.

The polite chatter was enjoyable, but I was too wrapped up in how close the proximity of Hayes' body was to mine to participate. My eyes kept fluttering to his large, tan hands. Hands that had pinned me in place and spanked me.

When we arrived, a thrill ran though me as Hayes again took the seat next to mine. A move that was not missed by my friends Georgia and Bridgette. Georgia gave me a curious eyebrow raise, and Bridgette flashed a brazen wink in my direction.

Food and drinks whirled around the table in a seemingly never-ending feast. Halfway into the meal, Bridgette filled my wineglass to the top from the chilled bottle of Pinot Grigio for a third time. My hand fluttered to my mouth as I giggled. My cheeks were already warmed from the wine.

Bridgette shrugged, her blonde curls bouncing around her shoulders. A naughty smile played on her lips, "You may as well finish it off, Louanne. Otherwise Georgia's going to go for it and get herself in trouble."

Georgia flipped her long shiny mane of dark hair over her shoulder, her hazel eyes flashing. "Give me a break, Bridgette—I can handle my alcohol."

Georgia's husband, Brody, gave her a sidelong glance from the corner of his eyes, his chiseled jaw tightening. "I'm going to side with Bridgette on this one, honey."

With a sigh, Georgia looked wistfully at her empty wineglass. "Well, then I call dibs on the last cannoli." She pierced the creamy concoction with her fork, stuffing a bite into her mouth. A smug smile crossed her lips as she indulged in the delicacy. "Sorry, Louanne. It's only fair."

"Fine with me, I'm quite happy with the wine," I said, taking another sip of the cool, tangy drink. It was delicious. Hayes had ordered it, knowing it was my favorite—and at the hefty price tag of thirty dollars a bottle, I was going to enjoy every last drop.

"I'm just surprised Bridgette's sharing so well," Travis said, a teasing glint in his dark eyes.

"Hey, I'm a generous person," Bridgette teased back, elbowing her husband in the ribs. "Plus, I'm a beer girl." Her nose wrinkled as she sniffed at her wineglass.

"An example of true generosity," Travis laughed.

Brody stood from his chair and tapped the side of his water glass with his fork. "And on the topic of generosity, I'd like to propose a toast." He lifted his glass in his hand, ice cubes clinking as he did. "To the staff of CLAS ranch. You all consistently give the best of yourselves to the ranch—your time, your talents, your energy. Without you all, there is no CLAS, just a few fields and buildings." His tanned, handsome face turned to me. He was a spitting image of country music star Luke Bryan, only with lighter, wavier hair. Georgia was a lucky woman and she knew it.

I smiled back at Brody, the man who had hired me years ago and was now more like a brother than a boss. My smile fell, my brow knitting in confusion as his attention remained on me.

"Louanne, this evening was, as I told you all back at the ranch, an evening to relax and show my appreciation to the staff for a job well done—and to eat a meal we didn't have to cook for ourselves with Memaw hollering at us." Everyone at the table gave a chuckle, Memaw laughing the loudest. "Cheers, Memaw!"

The laughter died down and his attention turned back to me, "But it's also an occasion to celebrate your hard work. You have been with CLAS since before you could drive a car. I've watched you grow both as a professional and a woman. Your creativity and attention to detail have helped to make our special events department what it is today. We wanted to take the time to thank you for the impact you have made. And now, Hayes would like to add a few words."

Brody gave me a nod. Feeling humbled by his kind words, I replied with a smile and lifted my glass with a quiet, "Thank you."

Beside me, Hayes stood from his chair. His blue-gray eyes looked over our team, flashing with emotion. Everyone quieted down, their attention focused on him. "Living and working off the ranch for these past six years, I learned a lot. But the most important lesson I've brought home with me, is just how lucky we all are to be a part of this. CLAS started as just a dream Brody had. But with the love, support, and hard work of family—and those of you that have become family—CLAS has become a place that turns others' dreams into realities. And one dream in particular— the most important day of a couple's life—a dream wedding." His gaze locked on mine, the corners of his mouth crinkling up into one of his rare, heart-melting smiles. "Luna, you create and implement those amazing weddings. You truly give people the gift of having one perfect day in their lives to celebrate their love. Coming back to the ranch and getting to work with you has been a pleasure. I may be your boss now, but every day I learn something new from you. You are a rare gem."

I gave a gulp. His words made tears sting at the backs of my eyes. But the way his gaze focused on my face—it took my breath away. This was Hayes—the boy I had known almost my whole life. When had he become the man who stood before me and made my heart pound against my ribs?

Hayes looked proud as his eyes rested on me again. "Tonight, we wanted to announce that thanks to Louanne's direction and the entire team's dedication, CLAS ranch has made it to *Travel and Dining* magazine's Top Ten resorts for destination weddings."

My eyes widened as I gasped. No ranch had ever made the *T & D*'s Top Ten. Those places were always faraway destination wedding resorts—white sand beaches in tropical paradise with the price tag to match. My hands flew up to my mouth in shock. A huge smile spread across my face, stretching my cheeks till they hurt. "No, way. Their Top Ten list? I had no idea! What an honor."

Hayes put a hand on my shoulder. "The magazine is coming out to interview Louanne and the staff. They are going to photograph the ranch and do a two-page spread on our weddings. This is really going to put CLAS on the map."

My friends looked toward me expectantly. I was not one for speeches. I managed to squeak out another meek, "Thank you." Hayes, knowing my dislike for public attention and making speeches, saved me by holding a glass up and calling, "Three cheers for Louanne."

He sat back down, his arm casually sliding along the back of my chair, brushing against my shoulders as it did. The skin beneath my shirt tingled at his nearness. My cheeks burned, my eyes cast downward as Hayes leaned over, whispering in my ear, "Great job, Louanne. You earned it."

"Not without yours and everyone else's help," I murmured.

He tucked a strand of hair behind my ear, leaning in closer. His husky voice whispered, "You're beautiful. You know that?"

I had no idea if it was the magic of the evening, or the Pinot Grigio running through my veins, but against my reserved nature, I brazenly slipped my hand underneath the crisp white tablecloth, and onto Hayes' muscular thigh. His eyes widened in surprise, a slow grin spreading across his face. His hand wrapped around mine, his arm tightening around my shoulders. "May I drive you home?" he asked.

"Yes." The word was out of my mouth before I could overthink it. Nervous butterflies tickled my tummy. Where would this lead?

• • • • • • •

Riding in the passenger seat of the car, I couldn't help but keep peeking over at Hayes. His gaze remained trained on the road before him. One of his large, perfectly formed hands held the wheel. His other hand held mine. His thumb brushed back and forth over my skin. My mind could barely process what was going on between us.

This was Hayes. The boy next door—if your next door is hundreds of acres of rolling cattle ranch. My friend, my boss, my innocent crush.

When I was being completely honest with myself, I could admit that I had always harbored feelings for him. He was so serious, so steady. Always calm and collected. Balanced with just the right amount of softness. And he was sexy. With that tanned, tight body and those gorgeous eyes, he was quite a catch.

And now, he was pulling into the driveway of my house.

Cutting the engine, he turned to me, giving me another one of those smiles. They seemed to be becoming less rare as the evening went on.

"May I walk you to your door?" he asked, giving my hand a gentle squeeze.

"Of course," I answered.

His eyes lingered on my face for a moment. His hand slipped from mine. With the grace of a panther, he slid from his seat, exiting the car and shutting his door behind him.

It had been so long since I'd been alone with a man like this. What was the proper protocol? Should I sit and wait for him to open my door in a chivalrous display of manhood? Or throw the door open myself, proving my independence? Before I could make up my mind, my door was swung open. Hayes was by my side, offering me his hand.

I slipped my hand into his. Tingles danced across my palm. I stepped out of the car, letting Hayes lead me up the path. We reached the front door of my little cottage. Facing one another, Hayes took my other hand in his as well. Standing underneath the soft glow of the porch light, the magic of the evening seemed to weave its way around us, binding us in its spell.

Hayes looked down at our joined hands. His thumbs brushed over the backs of mine. An uncertainty flashed within his eyes. He hesitated before he spoke. "Louanne, I have a question I've wanted to ask you since fifth grade."

My heart leaped from my chest. What could it possibly be? I'd never seen the look that rested on Hayes' face as he spoke. Nerves danced in my stomach as I replied, "What is it?"

"May I kiss you?" he asked.

Nerves turned to butterfly wings fluttering through my middle. My breath caught in my throat. I whispered, "Yes."

Hayes slipped his hand from mine. He slid it behind my head, tangling it in my hair and pulling my face toward his. Our eyes closed as I stretched up on tiptoe. My mouth met his. His arm wrapped around my lower back as his hand pulled me in closer. My lips parted, my tongue slipping into his mouth. My nipples tightened against my bra. My core melted, my entire body turned to jelly. Tingles vibrated over my lips as the kiss deepened.

Too soon, Hayes pulled away. He held my face in his hands, his soft eyes looked over me. He leaned in, placing one soft, parting kiss on my lips. "Good night, Louanne."

"Good night, Hayes."

He watched me as I let myself into the house. I waved from the window as he made his way down the steps to his car.

My fingertips brushed my lips. They still tingled.

• • • • • • •

Morning came and with it came the shock of what had happened. Hayes had kissed me.

Lying in my bed, I couldn't remove the permeant smile that had been attached to my face ever since Hayes had kissed me. I pulled back the mounds of feather comforters I couldn't sleep without. Tiptoeing over my plush white carpet, I hurried to the shower.

Stripping off my pink cotton nightgown, I blushed with shame. My nipples were still peaked, hardened from the memory of the arousing evening. Sighing, I stepped out of my still damp panties. I turned the shower on as hot as I could stand, stepping in and pulling the curtain behind me.

The hot water ran down my back, relaxing my muscles. I closed my eyes, leaning my head under the steady stream of water. Carefully, I squeezed Argan oil moisturizing shampoo into my palm—the stuff cost a fortune and I didn't want to spill a drop. Using my long, manicured fingernails, I scrubbed the shampoo into my scalp. Suds gathered, cleaning my hair as well as my soul. I rinsed the bubbles from my hair, then combed in a detangling rinse that smelled like strawberry.

Facing the showerhead, I tilted my head to the side. The water ran over my neck, my shoulders, my breasts, my stomach. The pelting of the water further awoke my nipples as they tightened. Thinking of last night's kiss sent a delicious shiver through me.

As the water cascaded over my skin, my mind wandered to the day ahead. How should I act around Hayes? Where did we stand after the kiss?

I could try to keep a comfortable distance from him. Be professional. But it was kind of hard now that he was directly over me. *Yikes*. If Travis' wife Bridgette had heard that, she would have chimed in with a giggle and her favorite joke, *that's what she said*. Cue a daydream; Hayes, hard as a rock and directly over me. The muscles of his shoulders tense as he hovered ready to slide that magnificent cock—

Back to daylight and working with Hayes. He was a great boss; firm but laced with just the right amount of softness— he even made everyone on the ranch homemade ice cream whenever they asked. And he was sexy. With that tanned, tight body and those gorgeous eyes, he was easy to look at during a long day of work. The way my pussy had responded to him when he had spanked me—it sent such a carnal longing running through me—it was going to be hard to stay focused at work.

Even before the kiss, I knew he was interested. According to Memaw, he had been since grade school. More than once, I had overheard her saying, "Hayes is as sweet on that Louanne as a black bear is on honey."

So, why—after a multiyear dry spell in the dating department—wasn't I jumping right on top of the opportunity to date Hayes? Or, as Bridgette would say, 'jumping right on top of Hayes.'

There were two itty-bitty issues that stood in the way of me taking a chance on love with the handsome cowboy.

Number one, Hayes was my boss. I prided myself on my professionalism and the fact that I grew my career from such a young age through hard work and maintaining a mature demeanor. Dating your boss did *not* fall under the category of things a professional woman did.

Issue number two; Hayes is a daddy.

As in, his women call him daddy, he calls them baby girl, and *he spanks his women.*

Someone who was more comfortable with her sexuality might say to me, "Louanne, what's the problem? Sounds amazing. Who wouldn't want that hot cowboy smacking their ass? Go for it, girl." And after last night, why not enter that kind of relationship?

But I just couldn't.

*I'm not that girl.*

Even if I could get past the fact that Hayes was my boss—I loved my job and would not do anything to put it in jeopardy—I had serious hang-ups about being with him.

I was the good girl. I had *always* been the good girl.

I took my mom out for lunch and manicures every Saturday. I still sent birthday cards—paper ones, through the mail. Not the ones you can make and send over email. I cleaned my house every week. I cooked fresh, healthy food for myself whenever I wasn't eating on the ranch. I donated to every charity that was requested of me, even the one where you had to buy wrapping paper from the little kids in town—I had a closet full of the stuff. I went to church every Sunday. I even taught the eight-year-olds' Sunday school.

When all my friends were making out behind the bleachers in high school, I was tutoring struggling freshman in the library. I was the girl who had saved her first kiss for her long-term college boyfriend—the one who turned out to be my last, and only, boyfriend.

I just wasn't the woman who entered a taboo, daddy/baby girl relationship. I was a strong, independent woman who liked doing things my way and not answering to a man—*especially* a spanking man.

But damn, that kiss.

Heaving a sigh, I shut off the water.

Hanging up the towel over the bar to dry, I hurried through my routine—there was a wedding to prepare for. I needed to forget about last night and focus on my very last to-do list. Still, nervous excitement danced through my belly as I dressed, knowing I was only an hour away from seeing Hayes.

Shoving thoughts of his lips against mine aside, I sat down at my desk, pulling my notebook from my bag. For every wedding I planned, I gave that wedding a nickname. The nickname always revolved around the theme, or something that had happened during the planning process. My notebook was full of lists of ideas, to-dos, as well as notes of what worked well—or didn't. My pen made scratching sounds as I furiously wrote the final list for the wedding that would take place this evening. This list was meant for my sister, Josie, who was currently working on the ranch part-time to help with events.

*Josie's Final Checklist for Friday Night Shoestring Budget Wedding*

☐ Make sure Colton is the one to help Lady DJ unload her equipment. (Since the couple couldn't afford a DJ, she offered to do it for free in exchange for lessons with Colton. I think if she gets a little eye candy before the ceremony she won't be upset when the wedding party inevitably does not tip her.)

☐ Call the bakery this morning to confirm, for the second time, that they will deliver the sheet cake at two p.m. (Do not, I repeat, do not do that thing where you say you are 'just taste testing the icing,' taking a little sweep from the bottom with your finger. I *saw* your trademark swipe at Overprotective Father of the Bride's wedding.

☐ Make sure the mother of the bride gives you the heirloom cake knife and server. Wear the white gloves (I'll know if you don't) and wipe any fingerprints from the silver. Put the servers and the gloves into the plastic bin marked 'Cake Server.' Please put the box in my office.

☐ I already have the hall decorated but we need to get

the heart ornament favors from the bride's aunt and place those on the table. Remember—spread the red. Do not lump them together.

☐ Brody does not like to be bothered on wedding days unless it is a true emergency. He has enough on his plate as it is. He will need to sign off on the purchase orders, but that is it! As soon as you get his signature, leave him alone. Do not tell him about how cute the delivery boy was or good the cake smells.

☐ Do not, I repeat, do not talk to Memaw when you go into the kitchen to start bringing the food out. And do not taste-test any of the food, Josie. I'm serious. Memaw is only to be spoken to after all foods are displayed. Remember, it will be buffet style as we cut costs on staffing.

☐ Be sure to have Lady DJ announce the tables one at a time to go to the buffet. This is a wedding, not a Black Friday Sale at Macy's. We do not want a stampede of hungry guests.

☐ Be sure to mingle as the guests eat and ask if they are enjoying the meal. I know they didn't pay for service but if you have time, fill a few glasses of tea to make them feel special. (Be friendly but not flirty. I know you can't help it because you're so dang cute, but I do not want to see a guest running his finger over the outline of your Mickey Mouse tattoo like I did at the Navy Seal Marries a Prom Queen wedding.)

☐ Just a reminder: Dim the lighting when Lady DJ switches over from the elevator dining music to the dance songs. Last time, you didn't hit the lights until we were two verses into 'We are Family.'

☐ Brush your hair. Though your messy bun is adorbs, it is *not* professional. Thank you.

I could picture my sister rolling her eyes as she read my

list. I knew she thought I was extra. A little overkill. But, in the end, when it came to weddings, I was always right. I placed my notebook in my bag and threw my bag over my shoulder. It was time to go.

# CHAPTER TWO

As soon as my boots touched ranch soil, last night's kiss was quickly forgotten. The workday was a whirlwind preparing for the wedding. I was in my element and the hours slipped by like minutes. Still flying from the high of hitting the magazine's Top Ten list, I worked away making my client's dream a reality. Once the barn was finally decorated for the ceremony, I stepped back to take in my work.

Everything was perfect.

Rows of white chairs were set up on either side, creating an aisle down the center of the barn. A white runner ran from the barn doors to the platform we had built. Okay, not 'we' exactly. I had shown Hayes the plans, and he had built it while I handed him tools. And he had looked damn good swinging a hammer with a tool belt around his waist.

A long table stood on the center of the platform. A white table runner with pink rose petals stretched across it. A filmy gauze weaved its way around a line of fifty-four white LED-battery-operated candles of varied sizes and shapes. I would turn them on via remote control just as the guests were arriving. Convenient, gorgeous, and… safe. I wasn't ready to admit that Hayes had been right about switching the candles.

Front and center, where the bride and groom would stand to exchange their vows, I had discreetly marked the floor with a taped *B* and a *G*. Just one of the touches I picked up over the years to help the day run smoothly.

To the right and the left of the marks were pillars with tall vases of white roses that were so pretty you couldn't tell they were fake. I had even dabbed several teardrop-shaped dots of hot glue on the petals to emulate dewdrops. Normally, I use our local florist for fresh flowers, but a few months before the wedding, our bride had come to me in tears, explaining that her father had some unexpected bills come up and had to cut her budget in half.

I calmed her down. The steaks changed to chicken, the fish to a vegetarian pasta. I bought the fake flowers myself. I could reuse them for Hearts on Fire—our romantic couples getaway that took place over Valentine's weekend. The LED candles I borrowed from Alice's stash that she had saved from the annual Christmas Eve bash. As the proud mother of the four Jenkins men, she was one of my favorite woman and I loved when she helped out with the weddings.

Josie had even found a cute female DJ who volunteered her time in exchange for private riding lessons from Colton (he had his hands full these days with admirers). I had managed to pull off the wedding of our bride's dreams and still stay within half of her original budget.

Taking a deep breath, I crossed my arms over my chest. Why not get the full effect? Pulling two little white plastic remotes from the pocket of my skirt, I clicked on the candles. Then the stereo. Soft music began to play, echoing through the empty barn. It was all so beautiful. The white lights twinkling, the classical music playing in the background. I thought of Memaw, busy in the kitchen bossing her crew around to get the food just right. Later, there would be dinner and dancing in the Mess Hall—also decorated to perfection if I do say so myself—followed by a vanilla buttercream cake with roses made of pink icing.

It was a dream wedding.

It was *my* dream wedding.

Would I ever tire of making the dreams of other women come true? Surely, one day I would have a wedding of my own, right? Float down a petal-dotted aisle in a white gown, headed toward the man I would spend the rest of my life with.

Who was I kidding—I barely had time to shower, let alone date. I was going to grow old on the ranch, planning other people's weddings for them while I became an old maid. Feeling a little sad, I slipped the remotes back into my pocket. I gave a heavy sigh, murmuring to myself, "Always the wedding planner, never the bride." Giving the candles one last glance, I turned to leave the barn.

"Oompf!" I cried, running smack dab into what felt like a wall—a warm, muscular, soap-scented wall. I looked up into the more-blue-than-gray-today eyes of Hayes Jenkins. His gaze locked on mine. A flutter lifted in my stomach as his hands grasped my shoulders, steadying me. His touch made heat course through my body, shamefully melting my core.

"Slow down, Luna." he said. His eyes caressed my face, lingering a moment too long on my lips. Memories of the kiss washed over me like a warm wave. Hands still on my shoulders, he asked, "You okay?"

A blush rose in my cheeks. I spoke too quickly, suddenly filled with nerves from his nearness as I replied, "I'm okay. Sorry—I didn't see you there." A deep heat radiated through my skin where his hands rested on my shoulders. Out of nowhere, the whispered taboo word 'Daddy' echoed in my mind.

My cheeks were burning. My pussy was pulsing. My panties were soaked. I forced myself to look up into his eyes. The second our gazes locked, I was at a loss for words. There was no denying it—the dynamic between Hayes and me had irrevocably changed. The innocent crush had grown into a carnal yearning. Fluttering my lashes, I lowered my gaze to the floor. It was all... too much. I had a wedding to pull off. I gulped down my emotions with a difficult swallow and managed to say, "I was just leaving... actually. Did you need something?"

Hayes leaned down, his lips brushing against my ear and sending a delicious tingle over the back of my neck, raising the tiny hairs to attention. His breath was hot against my cheek as he whispered, "Only one thing. *You.*"

My nipples tightened, straining against the constraints of my bra. My pussy clenched again, a gush of desire dampening my already soaked panties. I pulled away, looking up at him, shocked by his words.

Hayes didn't often smile but I noticed he seemed to do so more regularly since his permanent return to the ranch. A grin spread over his face. "But I'll find a way to put my needs aside and focus on the task at hand." Hands dropping from my shoulders, his eyes left mine. He crossed his arms over his chest, gazing over the barn and my handiwork. "I was just seeing if you needed anything, but clearly, you don't. Everything looks great. Really pretty. But I don't need to tell you that—it always looks great." His eyes were back on me, causing prickly heat to dance across my neck and chest.

"Thanks. I think it's one of my favorites that we've done." I stood next to Hayes, my eyes going back to my work. A heat radiated between our barely touching arms. I willed myself to ignore the invisible bubble of passion that seemed to envelop us. "And the candles were a good idea," I shyly admitted.

"Thanks. You only took a smidge of convincing." He raised a brow at me, making my cheeks flush. I trained my eyes before me, taking in the decorations. I could feel his gaze resting on me as he said, "It looks like you."

I further warmed from his compliment. I shrugged. "The bride and I have similar tastes, so it was easy to come up with something she would like."

"Every wedding you've done the bride has loved," Hayes said. "It must get old, always planning the wedding yet not getting to participate." My eyes widened, my mouth dropping open as I turned to look at him. Smiling, he shook his head, giving a sigh. "Always the wedding planner, never the bride."

Hayes had overheard my little pity party. How humiliating! His smile and his scent and his nearness and my embarrassment—it was overwhelming. Not to mention that looming elephant in the room, the kiss.

I needed some space.

I began to back away from him. With a wave of my hand, I stammered, "Oh, you heard that? Ha, ha. I was just joking around. I'd... I need to get back to work, now. I just have a few more adjustments and then," I took another step, "aaaaaah!" My heel caught the leg of one of the chairs and to further add to my humiliation, I began to make my descent toward the ground.

One long stride and an arm reach later, Hayes scooped me up, holding me against his chest. I half stood, half hung suspended in his arms. His arms surrounded me—he radiated heat like the summer sun—and his chest was pressed against me. Looking down at me—had he grown even taller since last night?—his gaze was cloudy with concern. He asked for the second time that day, "You okay?"

"Yes." I righted myself, wriggling from his hold. I brushed off my skirt, though I hadn't fallen and there was no dirt there. My eyes stayed on the ground as my cheeks burned, willing him to leave the barn.

Suddenly, a fingertip was under my chin, lifting my gaze to meet his. The place where his finger touched my skin sparkled with warmth. "You need a daddy to take care of you, sweetheart... I swear you're a danger to yourself, falling all over the place." He gave a chuckle.

"I can take perfectly good care of myself," I mumbled. "Hayes... we should talk... about last night. The kiss..."

"Best kiss of my life. I've been dreaming of it for over ten years, baby girl. And you don't always have to be the wedding planner, Luna. I'm happy to change that for you. Just say the word." With a wink, Hayes left the barn, leaving me standing with my knees shaking and my jaw dropped.

Hayes had me flustered. And if there was one thing I hated being when I was trying to pull of an event, that was flustered. Suddenly filled with nervous energy, I marched myself up the aisle to the front. My head shaking, I started straightening the already perfectly situated candles. As I worked, I murmured to myself, a habit that came up when I was nervous. "When did I become such a klutz? And when did Hayes get so tall? Did he always smell like that—that soapy, piney, manly smell? And what did he mean exactly? Was he offering to make me... a bride? That was *incredibly* unprofessional. I should tell him. Just because we've known each other practically forever—and yes, things are happening between us—does not mean that he can joke around about marriage proposals. Of all things!"

Throwing my hands on my hips, I took a step back to take one last look at the table. I gave a nod of satisfaction. I looked down to be sure there were no tripping hazards for me or my bride.

My eyes froze, glued to the ground. Directly centered between my feet was the letter *B*.

• • • • • • •

The ceremony went smoothly. Our blushing bride was grinning from ear to ear through the whole thing. The groom dabbed at happy tears as he declared his love through the vows he had written for his wife.

Dinner afterwards went as planned. The menu was a little more casual than I would have liked but when you are on a shoestring budget, you make do.

Lady DJ—as she had named herself—had an upbeat personality that the guests loved. Pulling my notebook from my pocket, I scribbled a reminder to call her on Monday to see if she would be open to becoming our exclusive wedding DJ. Her music selections were excellent, and both the bride's and groom's families were out on our parquet dance floor kicking up their heels. Which is something we don't often see at weddings. One side of the family usually dances while the other side looks on bored, or envious.

I hated to break up the party, but we were on a tight schedule as the couple could only afford to staff the hall for three hours. After an hour of dancing, we transitioned to the obligatory tear-jerking songs for the father–daughter and mother–son dances.

It was getting late—almost time to cut the cake and send everyone on their way. I gave the DJ my signal, spinning my finger in the air and mouthing the words 'wrap it up,' which meant cue the romantic music for slow dancing. It was one of my tricks—when the guests were having a blast, but the wedding had a hard stop time, we played songs that made everyone want to slow dance in one another's arms, or nod off to sleep, to get them ready to go home. She gave me a thumbs-up and started up a romantic number.

Folding my arms over my chest, I hugged myself. Watching the couples dance, a pang pricked at my core. One older couple in particular held my attention. The way they looked into one another's eyes, the way he held her as though she were the blushing bride.

Would I ever have that?

A hand lightly pressed into my shoulder, startling me. It was Hayes. My pulse quickened as I considered his handsome, kind face. His eyes were soft and a smile tugged at the corners of his mouth. "You did it again, Luna. Another wedding that will go down in someone's family history as one of the best days of their lives."

"Thank you," I murmured. As we stood quietly watching the crowd, I mulled over his words. "It's true, isn't it? That's why I love it so much. Helping to create a memory that will hopefully last forever." Feeling like what I had said was too heavy, I jokingly added, "Unless they get divorced that is."

His serious gaze fell heavy on me as he said, "I don't believe in divorce. When I get married, it's till death do us part, no matter what."

A shiver ran through me at his words. I stammered, "I didn't mean that I thought they would... I just meant that—"

"It's not something to joke about." One of his brows rose up toward the sky, his voice stern. I suddenly got the feeling I was in trouble with him.

"Okay," I answered, looking back at the dancing couples. A heaviness settled in my chest as I murmured, "It's just that not all love stories have happy endings."

"I'm sorry, Luna, I know it's hard for you to believe after what you went through but trust me. They're not all like... him." He placed a gentle hand on my lower back.

And I knew they weren't. I had seen how the Jenkins men were with their woman. Fully and utterly devoted. They would never up and leave their wife like my father had my mom. But even seeing good men firsthand couldn't remove all of the fear from my heart.

After an awkward moment of people watching, Hayes, standing rigid by my side, said, "Sorry to be so blunt. That's just how I feel about the matter."

"Noted," I murmured. "Hayes Jenkins does not believe in divorce. Let the future brides in the crowd know." I forced a laugh.

He turned to me, his gaze locking on mine. "There's only one woman in this crowd I would consider as my future bride."

My breath caught in my throat. I stared into his eyes. Was he serious?

He gave me a smile, holding his hand out toward me. "Care to dance?"

We had danced a few times in the past... Winterfest, prom, family weddings. But everything was different now. I froze. Hayes was my childhood friend. My off and on crush.

Yes, his tongue had been inside my mouth last night but sober dancing—that seemed more intimate than sex. Especially after the joke he had made this morning about me being his bride.

I placed my hand in his. When our skin touched, mine tingled. Did his?

Shyness overwhelmed me as Hayes led me onto the dance floor, our fingers intertwined. His arms wrapped around my lower back. Mine went to his neck, winding their way around as they had years before. He was so much taller now, his shoulders broad from hard work.

He smiled down at me. The pace of my heart quickened in my chest. We swayed to the music, him gently leading us as we danced. His gaze locked on mine. His voice was soft as he spoke. "It's good to be home."

*Home.*

I looked up at him, taking him in. His hold tightened, pulling my body to his. My breasts pressed against his muscular chest, my nipples hardening. I wanted to lay my head on his chest, to feel his chin resting on the top of my head. I wanted him to hold me like this for longer, call me Luna, or baby girl, maybe even give my cheek a gentle kiss. But the soft music floating through the night ended. Lady DJ's voice called out, "Please join us for the cutting of the cake."

The swaying stopped. Hayes' arms dropped from my waist. I untangled myself from around his neck. We were no longer touching, but our eyes remained locked on one another's. I could sense that great, passionate shift that now stood between us—a force larger than our relationship as friends, or boss and employee.

I stood speechlessly staring at Hayes as if he were an altogether different man. I could see in his blue-gray eyes what everyone had been telling me all along. Hayes Jenkins was in love with me. And I had feelings for Hayes. Dormant ones that had been hidden deep within me. Buried by time, distance, another partner. Feelings that now bubbled to the surface. Freed by one kiss and the magic of one dance.

As reality sank in, my breath caught in my chest. Hayes opened his mouth to speak, his soft gaze resting on me. "Luna, I—"

"Louie—cake time!" my sister, Josie, called from across the room. My eyes snapped over to where she stood, her arms frantically waving at me, her white-blonde messy bun bobbing on the top of her head. Apparently, she did not check off the final box on her list. Cupping her hands around the sides of her mouth, she gave a loud whisper, "I can't find the knife."

All romantic tension forgotten, wedding planner panic took over. Murmuring an apology to Hayes, I untangled my mind from his spell, spinning on my heels and rushing to my sister.

Breathlessly, I asked, "Josie did you look underneath the tablecloth? I always keep the cake-cutting knife hidden underneath the cake table. You know that."

My little sister rolled her eyes at me. "No kidding, Louie. This isn't my first rodeo. I checked—it wasn't there! You must have forgotten it!"

My eyes darted around the room, frantically searching for the clear plastic box marked, 'Cake Server.' The crowd had gathered around the table, making bets on whether the happy couple would smash cake into one another's faces. The bride and groom linked arms and were heading for their cake. In a matter of seconds, they would be standing at the cake table, the bride's family heirloom silver-plated cutter missing.

Where had I put it? I never forget to put the cake cutter under the table. Never.

There was a tap on my shoulder. "Looking for this?" I turned to find Hayes, holding the plastic bin in his hands.

"Thanks. Hold it for me?" I sighed with relief. Hayes held the box, watching me curiously as I carefully opened the lid. Removing the white glove from within, I slipped it onto my right hand. I reverently lifted the shiny knife and server from the box. I hurried over to the table, discreetly depositing the items on the tiny $X$ marks of tape and shuffled back into the shadows by Hayes. I quickly took off the glove and placed it back into the box. Hayes replaced the lid, murmuring, "Talk about attention to detail."

I smiled as my eyes trained on the happy couple. They held their hands together around the handle of the knife just the way I had shown them last week during my three-hour mandatory 'Bride and Groom Bootcamp.' I always held it the week before the ceremony to be sure they knew what would be expected of them on their big day. I also always requested Memaw fix them fried chicken for lunch, so they never minded.

"How'd you find the box?" I whispered.

"A magician never reveals his secrets." There was a twinkle in his eyes as he said, "Also… you left it in the office. I saw it in there just before the wedding, but I assumed you knew it was there. You never seem to forget anything."

Had I left it in the office? I meant to move it to the hall after I had finished decorating the barn but seeing Hayes for the first time after he kissed me had thrown me into a tizzy. In my flustered state, I had forgotten all about going to the office to get it and take it with me to the Mess Hall.

Hayes was right—I never forgot anything. This would never do. We had narrowly missed an absolute wedding disaster. A bleak spot on my career. What on Earth would have happened had Hayes not come out with the cake knife when he did? My stomach roiled at the thought of Josie running toward the couple, messy bun bobbing, yelling, "Here, use this!" and handing the bride a plastic butter knife. I shuddered. This would never do.

I was first and foremost, a professional wedding planner. And I could not let one fine-ass cowboy distract me into making mistakes.

"Hayes—we need to talk," I whispered beside me. His arm pressed against mine as we stood next to one another, watching the bride feed a dainty bite of cake to her groom. The heat from his body radiated into me, once again clouding my thoughts.

"What about?" he asked quietly.

Clearing my throat, I took a deep breath, preparing my speech and trying to ignore that delicious clean man smell emanating from him. "I pride myself in my work. And though last night was lovely, you're my boss now... things between us are..." What word could I use to describe that band of tension that ran between us and had me forgetting cake knives and wearing soaked panties all day? Things are... sexy between us? Smoldering, delicious, panty melting?

But it needed to come to an end. I just wasn't a baby girl kind of girl. It wasn't in me. And as much as I was attracted to Hayes, it wasn't fair to lead him on.

I took a deep breath. "Things between us are... weird. We need to maintain a professional demeanor if we are going to work with one another. What happened last night... can't happen again. Also, things like close, slow dances are off limits. As well as inappropriate jokes," I added.

His brow furrowed. "What joke?"

Giving an exasperated sigh, I said, "You know. The joke you made in the barn... the marriage proposal—"

Hayes turned to fully face me, his hand suddenly on my waist. His gaze locked on mine. I held my breath as he said, "*It wasn't a joke.*"

A buzzing filled my ears and my heart seemed to stop beating. White heat covered my face. A cheer went up from the crowd as the couple kissed.

The features of his face were etched in stone. The color of his eyes seemed to darken as he stared into mine. "I'm serious, Louanne. I'm in love with you. I have been for some time now—over ten years to be exact. Ever since that night of stargazing in the bed of my truck." My breath caught in my throat. Wordlessly I stood, staring up at him

His hands went to either side of my face. My cheeks tingled as his fingers wound their way into my hair. "Regardless of what happened between us last night, I'd marry you today if you'd let me."

Wordlessly I stood, staring up at him. He wrapped his arms around me as his face moved toward mine. My eyes closed. His lips were on mine, pressing against me. Time stood still for a moment and I allowed myself to return his kiss. A slow melting inched over my body as he held me, our lips joined. All thoughts of maintaining a professional, working relationship were forgotten.

He pulled away. His dusky gaze held mine. A smile spread across his face. "You have no idea how badly I've wanted you."

Fear be gone and taboo baby girl/daddy concerns be damned. It was time for Luna the moon goddess to replace good girl Louanne and be the woman who took what she wanted. And, I wanted Hayes.

"Me, too," I whispered.

Where did we go from here?

• • • • • •

"Get it together or forget it forever, Louanne," I demanded to my reflection. I had been messing with my hair for the past twenty minutes—which was utterly pointless as it was pin straight. I longed for volume, curls, anything other than... ordinary, which was what I had. At least the light brown had no gray—yet—and the bangs Beezus had cut in to frame my face looked pretty, but still, I longed for the beachy waves Bridgette got from just a few minutes with her magic hair iron. I had already spent ten minutes longer than usual dabbing concealer under my eyes and lengthening my lashes with mascara. It was nearing early summer, so my skin had a touch of color from the ranch sun. I pinched my cheeks, staring unhappily at my reflection.

What was wrong with me today? Scratch that—I knew

exactly what was wrong with me today. Hayes had declared his love for me. And we hadn't yet seen one another since his confession.

After our second kiss last night, he got called away by Travis to lend an extra hand. A cow was birthing and his usual assistant, Georgia, was under the weather. Casting me a glance over his shoulder, Hayes left with Travis.

Josie and I, along with the staff, cleaned up as much as we could. I dried every dish by hand, wanting to stick around and talk to Hayes after the kiss, but Josie was growing impatient and we had ridden to the ranch together.

On the drive home, Josie asked me more than once why my head was in the clouds, and why I had 'that weird look on my face.' I tried to make small talk about how pretty the bride was, or how did she think the food went over, but I was gone.

I dropped her off at my mom's house, then made my way to my cozy cottage. Pulling up to the little white house, I took a deep sigh.

The porch steps were dotted with potted flowers. The handmade wreath I had made last week hung on my bright blue door. The porch light shined, welcoming me home.

I went in, locking the door behind me. After showering, I laid in bed a long time, remembering the kiss and the way Hayes' body had felt pressed against mine. His words lingered in my mind: *I'm in love with you.* Lying on my bed had me even more wrangled up. My hair still smelled like him.

Eventually I fell asleep. My morning alarm had woken me up, puffy-eyed and messy-haired. Try as I might, I couldn't get myself looking good enough to suit me. Because, I knew I would be seeing Hayes.

It was as if the world now spun in a different direction. I had known him almost all my life. My time spent on the ranch with him had grown and changed over time, but now, it was completely different.

Hayes had declared his love for me. And he had kissed

me where other people could see. Staking his claim.

But could I be a baby girl?

I had always been a little intimidated by the devotion the Jenkins men gave their women. Yes, it was thrilling to watch. And I was envious of the protective way they doted on their girls. But I was also terrified by their dominant nature. I was an independent woman who liked to do things her own way and did not answer to a man.

But hidden deep inside me was a very strong urge to cuddle up on Hayes' lap and call him… Daddy.

I was so utterly, impossibly confused. Huffing a sigh, I gave myself one last long look. "Give it up, girl. It's time to go." I pulled on my worn cowgirl boots, smoothing my long skirt over top, grabbed a light jacket, and headed out the door.

The drive back to the ranch was surreal. I watched the sunrise over the hood of my little white Jetta, winding up the curving road to the ranch. As I drove, I talked to myself. "Louanne, you need to tell him that even though you may have feelings for one another, you've worked too hard for this job and you want to maintain a professional working relationship. Or… just tell him that you think you might love him, you want to make him your daddy and rip his clothes off and jump on top of what has to be a magnificent cock."

I parked the car and allowed myself one bang of my forehead on my leather-wrapped steering wheel. I took the last sip of my French vanilla creamer with a dash of coffee. Then, I got out to face the day.

The heels of my boots crunched over the gravel as I made my way to the office behind the Mess Hall. Mumbling to myself as I went… *remain professional… declare your undying love… keep your job… have his babies.* I put my key in the lock and turned it. The door easily opened without the usual jiggle I had to do—either the lock was acting up again, or someone else had already unlocked it.

I opened the door to reveal Hayes, seated at my desk.

His face brought back the memory of the kiss. His declaration of love for me. The spanking, the kiss, the dance, the… the word *daddy* whispered in my mind. Clearing my throat, I tried to assemble a cool composure. Overly conscious of my body, and how it may look to him, I walked over to the desk.

Hayes stood, stepping out from behind the desk and moving toward me.

"Hayes—" I started, ready to repeat the monologue I had crafted on the drive to the ranch. He took one last step, closing the distance between us. His hands went to either side of my face, cupping my cheeks. His eyes closed, and his mouth was on mine.

All words were erased from my mind. My knees went weak, my head lolling back. My lips parted, letting his tongue slip inside my mouth, exploring. His hands went to my jacket, undoing each button slowly. I shrugged out of the coat; it fell to the floor with a soft whoosh.

My arms wrapped around his neck, my hands running through his soft, short hair. He grasped my waist, squeezing my hips. Leaning up on tiptoe, I pressed into him. My breasts felt heavy, my nipples straining against my bra. He moved from my hips, caressing my back. One hand snaked forward, taking my aching breast into his hand. He cupped and squeezed, gently. My nipples further hardened. A soft moan escaped my mouth as we kissed.

Hayes' hands returned to my waist. They circled me, lifting me. I giggled as he turned me around, setting me up on the desk like a doll. I sat on the edge of the desk, my legs parting as his thighs pressed between them. His hands went to the back of my neck, tangling in my hair. Tingles ran from my neck down my spine. His mouth found mine once again. He kissed me hungrily. My core melted. My pussy clenched. My panties were wet.

The smell of my arousal from underneath my skirt reached me as his hands went to my bare knees. My breath caught in my throat. Goosebumps rose on my skin as he made his way up my thighs. Then, his hand found my pussy. Over my damp panties, he ran two of his fingers, pressed together. Up and down over my panties, stroking my clit. I shivered, my knees trembling.

His other hand went to my lower back, pressing me further in toward him as his fingers moved quicker. Breaking away from his kiss, I turned my head to the side, letting a moan escape my lips. His mouth went to my neck, licking and biting. His fingers found their way underneath the elastic waist of my panties. Exploring through the tendrils of my curls, his fingers dipped within me, collecting my juices. His slick fingertip found my clit once more, rubbing and stroking.

My hips gyrated, my ass pressing into the wood desktop. I grabbed the back of his head, pulling him in toward me. My mouth was on his. My tongue darted between his lips, the craving and passion in his kiss deepening with each stroke of his expert hand. My pussy tightened and clenched.

His fingers slipped from within me and went to the waistband of my panties.

I froze.

I pressed the palms of my hand into his chest. I pulled my head back away from him. "Hayes. I—"

His eyes focused on mine. "Luna—I'm sorry." His hands found their way out from under my skirt. Embarrassed, I looked down at my lap, smoothing the material. I waited for him to speak again. "I got a little carried away. I shouldn't have…" He trailed off.

Kissed me? Sat me on the desk? Fingered me? Tried to take off my panties? What could he say… I had wanted him to do all that he did and more. But things were moving too fast. In one night, Hayes had gone from childhood crush to almost lover. And I was still the good girl. And as much as I wanted to sleep with him, I didn't want the first time to be a wham, bam, thank you ma'am on my desktop.

My eyes locked on his. I cleared my throat and said, "Hayes. I need to slow down." A whoosh left my lungs. I read his face for a reaction.

His brows sprang up in surprise, his eyes widening. Before he could begin the long apology I knew was coming, I hopped down from the desk. "I don't want you to apologize for anything that happened. It was my decision too. I just need some time to sort out my emotions."

Closing his mouth, he gave a nod. "I respect that."

"I'm sorry, I just... it's a lot happening really quickly and—"

"Take all the time you need. You, Louanne Dixon, are worth the wait. Every second of it, baby girl."

Shivers ran through me at his gentle words. I had no idea what to say.

The ringing of my phone startled me. I used the opportunity to compose myself, picking up the receiver and saying a cheerful, "Louanne Dixon, event planner." Hayes gave me a long look, a tight grin, then left my office.

The door shut quietly behind him. I let out an enormous exhale of breath and plopped down in my chair. Trying to focus on the client's concerns, I half listened, my mind in a dream-like state. A smile slowly spread across my face. I had a feeling my multiyear dry dating spell had ended abruptly. My hand swept over my desk where Hayes had sat me down, the memory of his hand in my panties sending chills down my spine.

Luna the moon goddess.

• • • • • • •

The staff were gathering in the Mess Hall for lunch. Memaw was already dishing up enchiladas when I arrived. A blush crept into my cheeks when I saw Hayes seated at the table, an empty chair beside him. Quietly, I snuck in next to him, sitting down.

"Hey, baby girl," he whispered to me, flashing me a stolen smile.

*Baby girl.* The words made me melt.

"Hey, yourself," I murmured back. My hand brushed over my tingling lips. I wanted to kiss him again. Underneath the table, his hand rested on my knee. My skin tingled with warmth from his touch.

Memaw stopped in front of me, holding the pan in one hand and a spatula in the other. She gave my face a long, hard stare. A blush crept into my cheeks—I felt like she could read every emotion on my face. After a long, hard look, she gave Hayes a nod, saying, "It'll stick. And it's about damn time, too." Digging her spatula into the dish, she slapped a chicken enchilada down on my plate. "Not a moment too soon. I was beginning to think poor Hayes would die a bachelor. Death by unrequited love." Cackling, she went off to the next plate.

My face burned. Had everyone in the Mess Hall heard her? There had been whispers about Hayes and me around the ranch as long as I could remember. People were not going to allow us to quietly and privately figure out what was going on between the two of us. They would make it a family affair. Having Memaw—who had absolutely no filter—call us out in the middle of staff lunch was exactly what I didn't want.

Georgia's mouth dropped open. Looking from Hayes to me, then from me to Hayes, she said, "Are you kidding me? It's finally happening? After all these years?"

Bridgette showed up with Lila Bell on her hip. "What, Georgia? What's happening after all these years?"

Georgia looked to me to confirm Memaw's words.

I said nothing.

"Mind your business, G. Or I'll tell Brody you're starting rumors again. That didn't go so well for you last time." Hayes gave her a threatening look.

That shut her up. When Bridgette first arrived in Little Peak, Georgia had gotten herself into trouble starting a rumor that pertained to Bridgette's dating life. It was water under the bridge now, but they all still liked to tease Georgia about it. Georgia's pretty mouth closed, a blush rising on her cheeks. Bridgette hid her mouth with her hand, giggling behind it. Lila Bell mimicked her mother, giggling as well. Giving me a wink, Bridgette took off toward the drinks table, calling over her shoulder, "Yeah—that didn't go over so well with Brody. Did it, G?"

Brody sat down beside Georgia. "Did I hear my name?" he asked, smiling and showing his perfectly straight bright white teeth. Hayes and asked, "Is it true? What Memaw said in the kitchen?" He nodded toward me. "'Bout you and Louanne?"

"Why don't you let me and Louanne figure that out and we will get back to you all." Hayes' tone said there was to be no more discussion on the matter.

"Suit yourself," Brody said, scooping up a bite of his enchilada. "But when that announcement comes out, it'll be a pretty big day on the ranch. Might even have to throw a party to celebrate."

"You forgot to bless the food," Hayes said, obviously ready to get the attention off whatever was going on between the two of us.

Brody gave him a wink. "You're right, little brother. And we have a lot to be thankful for today."

The rest of the meal went more peacefully. There were a lot of sidelong glances and open stares at Hayes and me. I did my best to eat, but between the additional attention and Hayes' hand on my knee, I couldn't.

· · · · · · ·

Every day after lunch I went to the ladies' room to wash my hands and freshen my lipstick—Bridgette always teases me, calling me 'prissy.' So today, of course when I stepped into the communal bathroom, Bridgette and Georgia were already in there, waiting to corner me for information. I had to laugh, as Georgia begged, "Tell us, Louanne—pretty please?" Bridgette chimed in with, "It's only a matter of time before the cat is out of the bag. Josie already told us you two were slow dancing at the wedding."

Georgia's cheeks blushed prettily as she said, "I heard there was a kiss."

Should I play it cool? Act demure? Deny? Excitement filled me as I gushed, "There was a kiss. And he told me he loved me." I would keep everything else a secret... for now.

Their eyes widened as they gave a collective gasp. I laughed, enjoying the shock on their faces. "Details, Louanne," Bridgette demanded. "We need details! Are you guys, like official now?" The two women crowded in closer, waiting for me to spill the beans. Honestly, after the emotional whirlwind of the last few days, it felt good to have some girl talk.

How much to reveal? "I don't know... it's been weird ever since Hayes came back on the ranch. I mean, we've always been friends and there were feelings there on both sides at times—"

Georgia jumped in excitedly, "Girl, that boy has been in love with you for years. I've had to listen to his brothers tease him about it every time we go to Bud's—"

Bridgette elbowed her. "Shush, Georgia. Let her tell the story."

I continued. "Anyway, he's my boss now, which makes it weirder. Last night I was prepping for the wedding and I said, 'always the wedding planner and never the bride.' He overheard me and told me that he could change that at any time if I wanted."

"He threatened to fire you?" Georgia gasped.

Bridgette rolled her eyes. "No—he offered to take care of it for her. As in make her a bride."

"Oh. Gotcha," Georgia said.

"So then, he asked me to dance. And we've danced before but this time it just felt... different. You know?" I asked.

Both women nodded their heads, their eyes shining with memories of their own early love. "Then, I told him he couldn't joke like that—the marriage proposal joke—and he told me he wasn't joking and that he loved me, and that he would marry me today if he could."

A chorus of 'aawww!'s came from Georgia and Bridgette.

"And we kissed. And it was amazing. But then we both got busy and I didn't see him again till the morning."

Georgia chimed in, "Sorry about that—I wasn't feeling well last night and couldn't help out with Bessie. I hate to miss a birth—"

Bridgette blurted out, "What happened this morning? You two were sitting awfully close at lunch."

"I came in this morning prepared to tell him that we needed to keep things professional," I left out the part about his hands underneath my skirt, "but then he kissed me. And that's as far as we've gotten." I let out a deep breath.

"What are you going to do?" Bridgette asked.

"Honestly, I don't know."

Georgia looked from me to Bridgette, then back to me. Bridgette got a worried look on her face, as if she had read Georgia's thoughts. Georgia said, "Uh... Louanne, you've been on the ranch a long time—"

"Longer than the two of you put together," I said. I had a feeling I knew where this was going. If Georgia thought I wasn't in on the Jenkins men's way of life by now, she was more naïve that I already thought.

Bridgette interjected, "Right. So, you know?"

I held back an eye roll. "If I didn't know before you two showed up... which I did, and so did the rest of the town... then it would have been pretty obvious every time Georgia came out of Brody's office with a sniffling nose, rubbing her ass."

Georgia blushed. Bridgette giggled.

Turning to Bridgette, I said, "Or you, girlfriend, every time you say one of your dirty jokes and Travis gives you 'the look' and says, 'just wait till we get home.'" It was Bridgette's turn to blush.

Still, even though everyone knew that the Jenkins men

were spanking men, it was different when you might be one of the women they would be spanking on the regular. Sure, Hayes had spanked my ass for being mouthy. But officially dating a Jenkins man entailed a lot more than that. Softening toward my nosy friends, I said, "But, I do appreciate your concern, and honestly, it wouldn't hurt to have someone to talk to. You know… just in case Hayes and I were to… enter a relationship."

"We need to sit down and hash this out. Prepare you for life with a Jenkins man. Dive into your feelings and see where this thing is headed." Bridgette grabbed my arm. "Girls' afternoon out! Stat! I'll see if Alice would mind watching Lila Bell. This mommy needs a little girl time."

"Yes. Great idea, Bridge. Let's go to Bud's," Georgia said with a mischievous gleam in her eyes.

"Bud's? In the middle of a work day? I can't go out drinking!" I protested.

Bridgette gave me a hard stare. "You work too much, Louanne. Besides, it's a *Saturday*. All of the guests from last night's wedding will be checked out by three p.m. and we don't have anything on the schedule for tomorrow."

"Except church," Georgia said dreamily. She wasn't particularly religious, but Brody was in the choir and the man could sing. Since Brody had taken to doing solos a few years back, the female population of Little Peak had suddenly become quite devout, never missing a service.

"So, you have no obligations, you probably worked fifty or sixty hours this week, and with a possible spanking relationship on the frontline, you are in desperate need of girl time. Am I right?" Bridgette put a hand on her cocked hip.

I had to laugh. With her blonde curls, full ass, and sassy attitude, I could see why Travis enjoyed taking her over his knee. "Okay—you've twisted my arm. I'll go."

Georgia clapped her hands. "Girls' afternoon out! Let's go. I just need to tell Brody."

"Don't you mean, *ask* Brody," Bridgette teased.

"What about you?" I asked Bridgette. "Don't you have to *ask* Travis?"

"Bridgette has a lot more... freedom in her relationship than I do. Travis is more laid back than Brody is. But Travis is controlling in... other ways." Georgia covered her mouth, giggling.

Bridgette elbowed her in the ribs. "Save it for Bud's, G."

This was going to be an interesting afternoon.

Bridgette got Lila Bell settled with Alice. Georgia got permission from Brody to go. Bridgette put on her lipstick and black leather jacket. I went to find Hayes and tell him I was taking off.

His brow furrowed when I told him I was leaving the ranch for the afternoon. "Can we talk later?" he asked.

"Of course," I answered in a very professional— pretending his hand was not down my panties this morning—kind of way. I had to keep control of the situation. I was still in charge of my life, even though I had absolutely no power over my soaking, clenching pussy. Faking a cool demeanor—though my crotch was on fire, with butterflies tickling my stomach—I breezily said, "Feel free to call me later."

I drove Bridgette, Georgia, and myself to Bud's in the Jetta. The bar had only been open for the past couple of years and though I lived close, I had yet to go. I wasn't much of a bar person—if I had time and money on my hands I went to a salon—but it was fun to be out with the girls.

The place was empty—it was only four o'clock. We took a high-top table near the old jukebox. Bridgette said, "Pick your poison. I'm buying."

"I'll have a Pinot Grigio if they have any chilled. Otherwise I'll take a Cab. Thanks, Bridgette," I answered.

Georgia snorted. "It's Bud's, Louanne. He's got beer— draft or bottle."

"I'm afraid I'm not much of a beer drinker," I answered, trying my best not to sound prissy.

Georgia turned to Bridgette. "Get her one of those hard

ciders if he has them. I'll take a bottle of Bud."

"Check. One Miller Lite draft, one bottle of Bud. And one cider." Bridgette turned on her heel and went to the bar. The bartender smiled when he saw her. We watched as she ordered our drinks. A few minutes later, she was back, holding all three at once.

"Impressive," I said, accepting a bottle from her. The label said 'Hard Apple Cider.' I took a sip. It was delicious. Like carbonated apple juice. "I like it."

Bridgette smiled. "Good. Now finish that one because you are going to need a second one for the conversation we are about to have." She had already downed half of her pint.

I took another dainty sip. Georgia eyed me. What the heck? Why not? When in Rome. Holding the bottle back, I tipped my head, chugging a good quarter of the sweet liquid. I put the bottle down, wiping my mouth with the back of my hand. A huge belch escaped my lips.

A cheer rose up from the table. "Louanne—I didn't know you had it in you," Bridgette said, raising her glass to mine for a 'cheers.'

I giggled. "I don't, usually. I should warn you girls—I'm kind of a lightweight."

"Me, too. Which is why I'm only allowed to have two drinks," Georgia said.

I giggled. "Allowed? That sounds so strange. I mean—most women do what they want and don't have to check in with their partners. Or have their drinks numbered by them." I took another sip of my drink.

"Well, as you well know from working on the ranch for so long, in the Jenkins family, one does not 'do what they want.' The men are in charge in the relationship," Georgia said.

"Or your ass is grass," Bridgette interjected.

"I'm so used to doing things my own way. I've been single forever. I live alone. And until Hayes came back, Brody pretty much left me alone to do my job," I said.

"Right—but the key word you said was 'single.' If you

are with Hayes, you are no longer single, which means you will have to answer to him," Bridgette said.

As much as I loved and respected Hayes—and as wet as my pussy had gotten when he spanked me—I didn't think I could handle that type of relationship. I was an independent woman and did not want a man in charge of me, telling me what I could and could not do. Besides, I was a reasonable person. I made good choices. I didn't need a man spanking my ass—although that spanking in the kitchen really had improved my mood at work. Wrinkling my nose, I said, "Answering to someone else? That sounds terrible."

Georgia and Bridgette exchanged glances. Georgia placed her hand reassuringly over mine. "It's not. It's wonderful. Maybe we aren't describing it correctly. A spanking man isn't just spanking your ass when he feels like it—"

"But he does do that," Bridgette interjected with a wicked grin.

Georgia laughed, then continued. "He's so much more. He's doting and caring and cherishes you like you were the only woman on the planet. And his spanking is usually out of concern for your safety and well-being."

"And there is such a thing as a sexy spanking, you know," Bridgette added.

"Really? I always thought it was just a punishment thing," I lied, blushing and thinking about the one sexy spank Hayes had given me.

Georgia put her hand on mine, saying, "Oh, there are punishment spankings, too. Believe you me. I could not sit down all day last Sunday because Brody found out that I had accidently spent the cash he gave me for the church collection on beer with Bridgette the night before."

"But it was an accident," I said.

"Carelessness," they answered in unison. After sharing a laugh, Bridgette leaned in. "But back to the sexy spanks. They are the best. They get your ass all warm and tingly and make you practically ache to have him inside of you."

Georgia slapped her on the arm. "Bridgette!"

Bridgette shrugged, the shoulders of her leather jacket rising and falling. "What? It's true. My pussy is dripping after a spanking from Travis." She chugged the rest of her beer.

My face was burning. My ears felt like they were on fire. I had never, ever said the word 'pussy' out loud. Ever. Though I had experienced firsthand (excuse the pun) what she was talking about, it made me uncomfortable. I finished my drink.

Georgia hopped up from her seat. "I'll get the next round. Louanne looks like she needs another drink."

"Don't use your church cash," I interjected.

Georgia rubbed her bottom, laughing. "No kidding." She was over to the bar in a few strides of her long legs, her dark hair swishing behind her.

I was envious of how brazen Bridgette was about her relationship. She felt no need to apologize for who she was and what she liked. I was also made uncomfortable by her demeanor, and first instinct was to clam up. But I had questions. Lots of them. Plowing my way through my shyness, I asked Bridgette, "What did Georgia mean, back at the ranch, when she said that Travis is less strict but makes up for it in other ways?"

"Oh, that? Travis is my daddy," she said.

I was so glad my drink was empty. Had I been sipping it, I would have spit it out in shock. My brows rose. "Your… d-daddy?" No way! There was more than one daddy in the Jenkins brood? I knew all the men spanked but I had no idea there were other daddy/baby girls on the ranch.

"Yep. My daddy. My father is Dale Jones. And he's a damn good one. Love that guy. My *daddy* is Travis. Daddy as in daddy dom. I call him Daddy and he calls me baby girl. And spanks me and spoils me and takes care of me. And he likes to be in control—in and out of the bedroom," she said with a wink.

It was so taboo, so wrong, so… sexy. And I wanted to

experience it with Hayes. My pussy clenched in m
my clit pulsed. I was sure I would be changing my pa.
when I got home. "If you don't mind me asking, does Travis
spank you when you are... bad?" I asked. I couldn't think
of another word for it but it seemed strange to call a grown
woman 'bad.' I thought about Hayes taking me over the
island for my sassy mouth.

"He spanks me when I'm bad, he spanks me when I'm
good—hell, he spanks me when I walk into a room. My
daddy is an ass man and as you can see, I've got enough to
keep him busy for a while." She patted her round hip to
make her point. I laughed. Bridgette had a full, gorgeous ass
that I was envious of. I was average height, average weight,
average hair... average ass. But when Hayes looked at me, I
felt like the most beautiful girl in the room. And the way he
looked at me—didn't make me feel average at all.

Continuing with my line of questioning, I asked, "So, if
Brody is a bossy, strict spanking husband and Travis is sexy,
spanking daddy dom husband, what does that make
Hayes?"

She wiggled her brows. "Oh, Hayes is definitely a
daddy."

I widened my eyes, raising my brows in mock surprise.
"Really?"

"Yep. And if I had to guess, I would say Hayes is going
to be the strictest of them all. He has a very serious manner
about him. Don't you think?" she asked.

Strictest of them all? What would that entail? I wasn't
even sure I was ready for a full-time spanking daddy, much
less a strict one.

Georgia returned with the drinks, also managing to carry
all three at once. How often did they come here? Georgia
handed me mine. Holding up her bottle, she said, "Cheers,
to the first meeting of the Spanked Wives Club!"

Bridgette said, "Hear, hear! Cheers!"

I held my glass in midair, unsure what to say. "I... uh...
I've never been spanked (only a little white lie, right?) and

I'm definitely not a wife."

"Yet," Bridgette said.

Huffing, I asked, "What makes you so sure—"

Georgia said, "I heard Memaw say, 'it'll stick,' when she was talking to Hayes at lunch."

"Yes, but what does that have to do with anything?" I asked.

Bridgette leaned in. "Once Memaw says, 'it'll stick,' you'll be married within the year."

"Really? Who has that been true for?" I asked.

They both raised their hands in the air.

I took a long sip of my drink.

"And if I decide I don't want to be a spanked wife?" I squeaked.

"Have you seen the way Hayes fills out a pair of Wranglers? And those smoky eyes? Have you *had* his homemade vanilla ice cream? You'll come around. I'm sure of it," Bridgette declared.

Georgia giggled. "Besides. I love getting spanked. It's so… hot."

The question that had been plaguing me finally came to the surface. "Does it always hurt?"

"Yes… if you are in serious trouble. It does. But you won't get into too much trouble. You're a good girl," Bridgette said.

"I don't see you stirring up too much mischief. Although—" Georgia wrinkled her brow, considering me for a moment. She had known me longer than Bridgette. After contemplating, she answered, "You are kind of uptight. And a little bossy. I don't think that will bode well for you in a relationship with Hayes."

Bridgette took a gulp of her drink. "You can get kind of worked up, Louanne."

"I do not," I protested.

Georgia wrinkled her nose. "You are a little… prissy. You like everything a very particular way—"

"And sometimes you get mad at us if we mess it up,"

Bridgette added matter-of-factly.

"I do not," I repeated. "And I am not prissy." I looked down at the bottle I held. My pinky was sticking out as I prepared to sip my drink. Bridgette eyed me. I clamped my pinky firmly to the glass.

Georgia put her hand over mine, saying softly, "We like you just the way you are. I'm just saying that it might cause you some friction with Hayes."

"Why would it cause friction with Hayes? It's just me, doing my job and telling everyone what needs to be done and when," I huffed.

Georgia shrugged. "If you enter a relationship with Hayes, he will have the final say on matters. And you *always* seem to like to have the final say. I'm just saying, I could see that causing some friction between the two of you."

"And Jenkins men resolve friction with one thing," Bridgette said.

"Spanking," I murmured.

"Bingo," Bridgette said.

I could be a tad uptight. And yes, I was known to freak out on our employees from time to time for their silly screwups. But overall, I was easy to get along with. Wasn't I? There was only one person I trusted to give me an honest answer. My sister, Josie.

# CHAPTER THREE

Snuggling into my mom's couch under my favorite afghan we'd had since I was a baby, I looked at my sister. She sat on the floor across from me, flipping the pages of a magazine on the coffee table. Her bleached blonde hair was twisted up on her head in the cutest messy bun. The colorful tattoos lining her arms were pretty against her pale skin, each one added to the collection during a last-minute trip she had taken. She wore the comfiest looking sweatpants— ones I would not be caught dead in—and a tee shirt with holes in it from some rock band I would never listen to. She was my opposite. And the person I loved most in the world. The one who knew me best. Taking a deep breath, I asked, "Do you think I'm bossy... and... uptight?"

Not bothering to look up from the glossy ads, Josie snorted.

"What's that snort supposed to mean?" I asked.

"That snort meant yes. You are uptight," Josie said with a roll of her eyes, flipping the magazine closed and throwing it onto the coffee table.

"But I'm fun. I'm spontaneous," I protested.

She held out her fingers, counting my faults on them. "And you freak out if things don't go according to your plans. You boss everyone around—which, don't get me wrong, it's the main reason the events go as smoothly as they do, but things have to be done your way." She gave me a curious look. "Although these past few weeks you've been a lot easier to work with. What's up with that?"

I gave an innocent shrug.

She rolled her eyes again. "As far as being uptight goes, you haven't dated anyone for two years! It's like instead of needing a guy, you get off decorating rooms with tulle and ribbon," she exclaimed.

My face burned.

A laughing twinkle entered her eyes. "Sorry, sis—did I take it too far?"

"No." It was true. I'd had quite a dry spell. Josie had slept with her first boyfriend at the age of fifteen, so it wasn't like I was trying to role model for my wild child younger sister. Why hadn't I dated in so long?

Josie's voice softened. "Louie, in all honesty, you get the job done. If you weren't uptight at work, you wouldn't be able to pull off the gorgeous events you do. And you make it look effortless. So, yes… you are incredibly bossy and very uptight, and we all love you for it. Why do you ask?"

"I… I… uh…" I stammered.

She lifted a brow, playing with the stack of jangling bracelets on her wrists. "Did Hayes say something to you? He seems like a pretty hands-off boss."

"But a hands-on boyfriend," I mumbled before I could stop myself. My hand flew to my mouth. Damn that second drink!

Josie laughed at me. "It's no secret, sis. I know Hayes and you have finally succumbed to your feelings for one another. I saw the kiss Friday night after the cake cutting. I tried to get you to talk about it on the ride home, but I could tell you weren't ready. You and Hayes are a perfect match. And now that the time is right for the two of you, you need to face the facts."

"What facts?" I asked.

"You are going to be getting spanked… sooner than later," Josie said.

I was mortified. My head fell into my hands as I wailed, "Josie—what am I getting myself into?"

She shrugged. "Don't ask me. I've been trying to get Colton to spank me for a year now. Every time I'm working on the ranch, I try to be sassy, or bend over a table, just so…" She hopped up from her spot on the floor, demonstrating for me over the coffee table. Her sweatpants-covered bottom wiggled in the air, making me laugh.

"I don't think that's how it works," I said.

"Still, I try," she said, plopping down beside me on the couch. She tugged half the afghan off me, covering herself up.

I asked, "Did you know Bridgette calls Travis… Daddy?"

Josie rolled her eyes. "Like, for over a year now. What planet have you been on? I swear—all you do is work. You need a vacation."

How had I missed that? Maybe I *was* too involved in my job. Josie continued, "I sure hope Colton is a daddy. Yummy," she said, licking her lips. "That man can be my daddy any day—"

I held up my hand to stop her. "Enough, Josie."

"See—you are uptight. Case in point," she sniffed.

I protested, "I don't like hearing you talk about Colton that way. You are my little sister, and he is like a brother to me. You've only been working on the ranch for two years… you need to maintain a professional composure. Which does not include trying to get the boss' brother to… spank you."

"Fine. Enough about me. But man, you and Hayes? Finally? I can barely wrap my head around it. He's been in love with you since what… fifth grade? I can't wait to tell Mom when she gets home," Josie said.

I said, "Don't you dare. I haven't even made it official

with Hayes, yet."

"Then why are you sitting here with your sister? Go find him and get rid of your old maid status. Maybe even get yourself laid, finally. You'd be doing us all a favor... Miss Uptight," she teased.

"Josie Dixon! You ought to have your mouth washed out with soap," I said.

She wiggled her eyebrows. "Maybe you should tell Colton on me."

• • • • • • •

I sat in my mom's driveway, unable to make myself put the keys into the ignition. So much had happened in a short amount of time, and I needed to process it all. The spanking, the dance, the kiss, the conversation about daddies and discipline with Georgia and Bridgette, the chat with Josie, it was all starting to tumble together in one messy knot of emotions.

There had to be a way to sort out my thoughts. Or at least make myself feel like steady Louanne once more. Get back down to Earth and put my feet on some solid ground. There was one thing that always made me feel better when I was overwhelmed with wedding planning. And that was— making a list.

Pulling my phone out of my purse, I tapped in my password, 'wddngplnnr,' and opened the notes app. I would make a list. One that would outline what had changed between Hayes and me and how I felt about it.

*A list describing the course of events leading up to this constant fluttering in my stomach and how I feel about it...*

1. The spanking—I've wondered for a very long time how it would feel. It hurt way more than I expected! During the spanking there were so many emotions... lust, fear, pain. But it also made me feel incredibly... sexy. No denying that! Afterwards, it

grounded me at work and made me mind my manners. Overall it was a very positive experience.

2. The first kiss—this was the moment the lines really began to blur between Hayes and ne. How can you go back to being friends after a kiss that makes your knees turn to jelly? You can't—and I don't want to.

3. The dance—being in Hayes' arms like that... then him telling me he was in love with me! Everyone on the ranch has been trying to tell me how he felt for years. But coming straight from his mouth—my heart is still racing.

4. Baby girl—am I naïve to think there is no woman who wouldn't love a big, strong man to call them baby girl? The name makes me melt and feel all soft inside. I was already used to the pet name. And it made me want to call him Daddy.

5. Convo with the girls—I have mixed emotions about this one. Instead of making me feel better, I think our honest discussion may have created more fear about being with Hayes than excitement. I mean, in this day and age, is it really okay to be a... spanked wife? Will I lose my independence? Become a doormat? Or will I gain something?

6. Josie—what a brat. Calling me uptight, lol. But really, it sounds like she is the one who should be dating a Jenkins man! How I wished I knew what I want like she does and be brave enough to go for it. Or, to be as comfortable in my own skin as Bridgette is... that would be incredible. Then, there would be no question what I would do... march right up to Hayes and tell him this baby girl has found her daddy.

7. Which says it all, right? I want Hayes. The man who would love me forever... and never leave me. *Right?*

Sighing, I read over my list. It was no use. The truth was that this thing happening between Hayes and me couldn't be simplified by a numbering of events. I tapped on the little picture of the trashcan on my screen, and my list disappeared. Fumbling for my keys, I started my car and got on the road. I would just have to be patient, relax, and let our future unfold naturally.

Pulling up to my house, I was surprised to see the red ranch truck in my driveway. Taking my phone out of my purse, I checked my messages—nothing. There had been no emergency on the ranch, but it looked like Hayes was paying me a visit. A nervous knot formed in my stomach. Checking my hair in the rearview mirror, I gathered my things, leaving the car. When I walked down my drive, I saw Hayes, rocking on a rocker on my front porch. My heart lurched into my throat.

Why was he here? Were we going to have 'the talk'? And, which 'talk' would that even be? The 'are we boyfriend, girlfriend' talk? The 'things are weird between us since we kissed, and you declared you love for me the other night' talk? The 'how do we slow things down after years of sexual tension between us' talk?

Or, more important, would it be the 'are you going to spank me and be my daddy' talk. Taking a big breath, I braved my way up the stairs to Hayes. The words I had written for number six on my list echoed in my mind... *there would be no question what I would do... march right up to Hayes and tell him this baby girl has found her daddy.*

His hands rested casually on the arms of the chair as he rocked back and forth. His handsome face shone under the warm porch lights. "Hey there. You have fun with the girls?"

"I did. Thank you," I replied, sitting down on the rocking chair beside him. "How long have you been here?"

"Just a little while. The girls got back to the ranch a little while ago, so I thought I'd come by here and see if you were up for a chat. I thought you'd be home by now," he said.

"I stopped at my mom's on the way back—to talk to Josie. I had something I had to discuss with her," I said.

His brow furrowed. "Can I ask what?"

I took a deep breath. "When we were out at Bud's, Georgia and Bridgette told me I'm... uptight." I snuck a peek at Hayes' face. He was smiling. "I stopped to ask Josie if it was true."

"What did she say?" he asked.

I answered, "She didn't even reply at first. She just snorted. Which was a resounding 'yes.'"

"What do you think?" he asked.

"I don't think I'm uptight. I just think things need to be a certain way for everything to run smoothly." I hesitated, then asked in a small voice, "Do you think I'm uptight?"

He smiled again. "I think you're perfect. And there would be no events at the ranch if it wasn't for you and the way you run things. You just need a tiny bit of adjusting every now and then." He lifted his hand, bringing it back down on his thigh with a gentle pat.

A grin tugged at the corners of my mouth. "Thank you."

"What brought the subject up?" he asked.

White heat covered my face. My stomach was a bundle of nerves. So quickly we had arrived at the conversation I had been putting off... possibly the reason I had put off dating Hayes for years. Time to be brave, Louanne. I looked Hayes right in the eyes and said, "They were guessing the reasons that you would want to spank me, if you and I were to enter a relationship. And... whether or not you were a... daddy."

His smile was a full grin. It made my knees weak and my heart beat faster. He leaned in toward me, my pulse further accelerating. He asked, "Is that so?"

"Yes."

"I've already spanked you once for being sassy—and it worked wonders," he said.

I gave a shrug. My mixed emotions caused a cloud of confusion to rise up around the conversation.

"And why do *you* think I would spank you? If we were to enter a relationship?" he asked.

"I don't think I would let you," I said huffily. "Besides—I'm a grown woman and I don't *need* spankings."

He eyed me curiously. "But... do you *want* them?" He continued to stare at me in a way that made me feel I was sitting on my porch without a stitch of clothing on my body.

A fire burned on my cheeks. My pussy throbbed, my breasts ached, my nipples peaked. I wanted his fingers back in my panties. "I haven't decided," I answered.

"You can't decide if you want something or not. You just know it." His hand reached out toward me. His finger brushed over my hardened nipple as it made its way to my heart. "In here." Eyes trained on me, his hand left my breast, making its way down to my knee. Slowly, it slipped up my skirt. "And in here," he said. My breath caught in my throat, my head lolling back as his fingers pressed against my wet pussy. He began to rub, picking up where he had left off in the office. "Tell me, Louanne... do you want it?" My breath quickened. I rocked the chair back and forth, moving my aching pussy up and down along his fingers. His whispered words intensified the pleasure, my clit pulsing under his touch. "Do you want me to take you over my knee? Pull your skirt up over your bottom? Pull your panties down around your ankles? Spank your bare bottom with my hand? Tell you what a naughty girl you've been? Do you want me to be your daddy?"

My eyelids fluttered as I gazed at him. His eyes were heavy with lust. He licked his lips as he watched my face. His fingers moved faster over my panties. Closing my eyes, I rocked harder in my chair. There was a tightening within me as my clit felt as if it would explode. "I... I... ah..." I moaned, the words caught in my throat.

I gasped as an explosion happened within me. I shuddered, pushing at his hand. I could take no more. He leaned in, his lips brushing over my earlobe. "You will be mine. And you will be spanked." A shudder racked my trembling body. "And you will call me Daddy."

I couldn't speak, couldn't move.

took my hand, leading me into the house. As we ___ the corner, I gasped at the scene that awaited me. Dozens of tiny, flickering flames rose from white candles. Real wax candles that burned warm and filled the air with the scent of vanilla. They dotted the coffee table, my side tables, the mantel. A small fire burned in the fireplace. On the coffee table was a chiller full of ice, a bottle of champagne nestled within it. Two cut-crystal champagne flutes waited beside the chiller.

"Hayes. It's gorgeous." I walked over to the couch, taking a seat in my favorite corner and admiring the candles. No one had ever made such a romantic gesture for me before. I asked, "How did you manage this?"

"You left the door unlocked," he said with a frown.

"Did I?" I shrugged. I always left the door unlocked. It was easier to get back in.

He eyed me. "You did. And we'll be talking about that later." A thrill ran through me at the threatening way he raised his brow. "First, champagne."

Holding the bottle up, Hayes undid the cork, letting it go with a loud 'pop.' He poured the champagne into one of the flutes, handing it to me. I took it from him, waiting for him to fill his. He held his glass up, holding it to mine. "I propose a toast. To a lifelong friendship that has blossomed into love." We clinked glasses and took a long, slow sip of the cold, bubbly liquid. It was sweet, just like his toast, and it made me smile.

Nerves danced in my stomach as I shyly eyed Hayes. He was seated beside me, the candlelight dancing on his face. A smile tugged at the corners of his mouth. Leaning in, his hand tangled in my hair, wrapping around the back of my neck. His lips pressed against mine. The taste of champagne lingered on his lips.

"I don't want to rush you. You tell me when you're ready," he said.

His eyes locked on mine, his fingertips trailing down my cheek. His thumb brushed over my bottom lip, causing shivers to run down my spine. He tucked my hair behind my ear, his fingertips stroking my cheek. When he spoke, his voice was thick with emotion. "I've wanted you for so long."

My eyes lowered. A blush burned in my cheeks. Nerves filled my stomach and migrated into my chest. My heart skipped three beats as I wound my hands together in my lap. I was too shy to speak.

The tip of his finger was beneath my chin, tilting my gaze up to meet his. His eyes were warm as he questioned me, "Do you want me, Luna?"

Biting my lower lip, I gave a tiny nod. As much and as long as I had wanted this, fear took hold of me. Knots formed in my stomach. My knees were shaking. I pressed them together, hard, trying to steady them. His hand cupped my chin, bringing my face toward his. I closed my eyes as his lips met mine. My body stilled, my muscles relaxing. The kiss melted me from within. My nerves dissolved, leaving me. I felt as if I was floating. His lips pressed harder against me. His hands tangled into my hair. My arms found their way around his neck.

The very tip of his tongue slipped into my mouth. His quiet exploration of my mouth made my pussy liquid and warm, my core flowing with lava. His large hands wound around my waist. Lifting me, he pulled me onto his lap. His hands caressed my back, moving up my neck and once again tugging on my hair.

I opened my mouth further, sliding my tongue into his. Our mouths moved against one another's, deepening the melty, sensual calm that was taking over my body.

One of Hayes' arms scooped underneath my thighs, the other around my lower back. Still attached at the lips, he scooped me from his lap and up into the air as he stood from the couch. Pulling away, I laughed as he carried me like a bride over the threshold.

To my bedroom. My heart pounded hard in my chest. I had never had a man in the bedroom of this house before.

Nerves fluttered in my stomach as I quickly counted how many months I'd been celibate. It was too many to count.

In my room, my dresser was covered with the same vanilla pillar candles. Their tiny flames flickered in the mirror. I watched our reflections as Hayes carried me into the room. The soft lighting on our faces looked lovely, romantic. Calm flowed over me, my nerves settling. I was surprised by the sensual smile that rose on my face. Gently, Hayes laid me on the white piles of comforters and pillows. "Someone once told me LED candles were for people who didn't have enough class to light a real one. I wanted to show you just how much class I have." I laughed as he lay down beside of me. "Hey, you," he said, brushing my hair back. He considered my face. A small smile rose on his lips. "You are drop dead gorgeous. You know that?"

I smiled, unable to answer him.

He said, "You don't, do you? I guess that's my new number one job. Luna, moon goddess." He kissed my forehead. "Good thing that I'm up for a challenge."

Shyly, I admitted, "You already make me feel like the most gorgeous girl in the world. You always have."

"I've always known you were. I still remember you sitting there at your desk, eyeing me as the teacher introduced me to the class. I caught you watching me on the playground a couple of times. Then, as we grew older, I looked forward to holidays on the ranch—I just wanted to get home to see you," he said.

"What about your girlfriends? There was a long line of those," I teased.

"They were just distractions. While I waited for you to finally see you were meant to be with me. Do you know why I moved home?" he asked.

"Brody needed you. The ranch just wasn't the same without you," I whispered.

"It was something Georgia said," he said.

"Georgia?" I asked.

"Yes. She's been giving me a hard time ever since she

moved on the ranch—she knew how I felt about you from day one. She said she could tell just by the way I looked at you that I loved you. Anyway, over breaks and holidays, we would all go to Bud's. Everyone would tease me, asking me why I hadn't told you how I felt, yet. I ignored them. I lived out of state and you weren't exactly giving me any signals. Then, that Christmas that Bridgette came around, she was pretty blunt with me. So blunt, I actually didn't really like her when we first met." We both laughed, knowing Bridgette could be a handful. "She was constantly telling me to ask you out. Later, I was complaining to G about Bridgette not minding her own business. And you know what Georgia said to me?"

"What?" I asked.

Hayes drew lazy circles on my upper arm with his fingertip as he spoke. "She said, 'Hayes, Louanne isn't leaving this ranch. And if you don't tell her how you feel, you will always regret it. Come home. At least then, you will never wonder what could have been. You'll know.' I spent a few more months mulling over G's advice. I decided she was right. Then, the very next time Brody called me, telling me to come home and work on the ranch, to his surprise, I said, 'yes.' And, here I am."

My heart fluttered in my chest as I whispered, "You came back for... me?"

"Yes," he said.

I had no idea. When Hayes came back on the ranch, I—along with everyone else—had been delighted. But I had assumed he had tired of his corporate job. Or missed his family. Or was tired of Brody giving him guilt trips. It would never have crossed my mind in a thousand years that he had returned... for me. "But you had to quit your job... and move. And, go back to ranch work. Is that what you wanted?" I asked.

"I want you," he said.

"But that doesn't seem fair for you to have to do that," I said, overwhelmed by the sacrifice he had made.

He held my face in his hands. "Louanne, I don't care where I am or what I'm doing if I have you. And G was right—you aren't leaving the ranch. So, I'm not either."

"You would do that for me? Turn your whole life upside down?" I asked. Was I worth that? What was so special about me that Hayes would give up everything he had worked for away from the ranch?

"My life *without* you was upside down. Now, my life is right. I was living with a moon-shaped hole in my heart."

His words settled over me like a blanket. I couldn't speak. The urge to kiss him overtook me. I moved from where I lay on the bed, leaning over him and bending down. I pressed my lips against his, my hair fell in a curtain over our faces. "I love you, Hayes," I whispered.

"I love you too, baby girl. And now, I'm your daddy." Without waiting for me to speak, his tongue slipped between my lips. His hands grabbed my ass, his fingers digging into my flesh.

My nipples hardened. I pressed my breasts against his chest. I slid my leg over his, pressing my pussy against his muscular thighs as I breathed, "And a damn good one, too."

A grin spread across his face. His hands went beneath my skirt, rubbing my bottom over my panties. My hips gyrated, grinding my clit against him as we kissed.

Hayes' hands traveled up my ribcage, beneath my shirt. In one smooth motion, he had my shirt off and up over my head. He kissed my mouth, my neck. I leaned forward, and he unhooked my bra, freeing my breasts. I lifted the hem of his shirt, pulling it up over his muscular torso. He took the fabric from me, pulling the shirt over the back of his neck. I lay back down and he lay on top of me, his bare skin pressed against mine. The heat from his body radiated through me.

Our tongues intertwined. Then, his mouth left mine, his kisses trailing down my body to my breasts. His mouth moved to my nipple, taking it between his lips. Lightly he nipped it with his teeth. I sucked in my breath as shivers ran through me. His hand massaged my breast as his mouth continued to tease.

Then, his mouth was kissing my torso, making his way down my stomach. My hands went to his hair, my fingers running though his soft locks. He sat up on his knees, a lustful smile on his handsome face. A hungry look flashed in his eyes in the light of the candles. His hand went to my waist. He pulled my skirt and panties down as one.

I trembled as I lay, fully nude, under his gaze.

"So beautiful," he murmured. And then, his face was gone from my sight and nestled between my legs. I gasped as the tip of his tongue parted my slick folds. He licked up and down until I was groaning. Then, he circled my clit. My hips arched in the air, my clit begging him for more direct caresses. Finally, he gave me what I wanted. Closing his lips around my swollen bud, he licked and sucked. His mouth was warm and wet, and it was the most delicious thing I had ever felt.

Within me, my muscles tightened, my pussy gushing with sexy juices, preparing for his cock. My hips moved in rhythm with his mouth as the orgasm built. "I—I'm going to come!" I screamed. My entire body tensed. My muscles broke into a hard shudder as the orgasm rocked my body.

When my eyelids fluttered open, Hayes was above me. Slowly, he lowered himself on top of me. My hands caressed his muscular shoulders. The tip of his cock pressed against my wet opening. I bit my bottom lip so as not to cry out as his cock pressed past the tight entrance. Pain gave way to intense pleasure as he plunged his member deep within me.

I cried out then. He slowly pulled away, leaving me empty inside, begging for him to return. Again, he thrust within me, the walls of my pussy tightening around him. My hips rose to meet his, pushing him even further inside of me. In and out he rocked, each push bringing me closer to another earth-shattering orgasm.

Foreign little whimpers that sounded strange came from deep within me as I released, giving myself over to the unstoppable climax. Hayes pressed inside of me one last time. He came within me, an animal-like groan escaping his lips.

His forehead pressed against mine as we panted in one another's arms. We had finally done what our bodies had been telling us to do for years. And it was incredible.

•  •  •  •  •  •  •

How could I have possibly gone so long without sex? And sex with Hayes—I had no idea lovemaking could be so delicious, so intense. A rosy glow covered my cheeks as I sat up in my bed. Thoughts of the night before drifted through my mind. Hayes' fingers and lips, his words, his hands, all giving me intense pleasure.

I hopped out of bed, throwing my curtains back and taking in the sunshine. I was a new woman. One with a boyfriend. A hot, dominant boyfriend who liked to spank. I took a hot shower, almost sad to wash the traces of lovemaking from my body. Rushing over to my closet, I wondered what one wears to work the day after. Flipping through my cardigans and long skirts, nothing seemed quite right for a woman whose body had been ravished by her daddy.

Did I not own anything black? Suddenly my clothes looked like the wardrobe from the set of *Little House on the Prairie*—which made sense, I loved that show. Digging through my drawers, I tried to find something that looked more like Madonna and less like Ma Ingalls.

I finally settled on a pair of black work pants that were slightly tighter around the rear than I usually wore, and a white sleeveless high-neck shirt made of lace. I slipped on my black shoes. Looking in the mirror, I fluffed at my hair. It was slightly tousled from the night before, giving it a sexy morning-after look. A little eyeshadow, blush and mascara, and a touch of lipstick, and I was out the door.

My bag slung over my shoulder, I made it down the first

three steps before I remembered, "Oh, I have to lock the door! Or I'll be in trouble." The thought of Hayes' fulfilling the threat he had left me with last night—lock this door, or else—warmed my core and made my pussy tingle. Hopping back up the stairs, I dug through my purse, found my keys, and locked the door.

Back down the stairs, into the Jetta, and I was off.

To see my daddy.

• • • • • • •

Walking in to my office, I was delighted that Hayes, once again, sat at my desk. Dropping my bag in the chair, I walked over to him. There was a huge smile on his face as he stood to greet me.

"Hello, you," he said, wrapping his arms around my waist. My arms went around him. Reaching down, his kissed my lips.

"Hello to you, too." Heat rushed through my body as his kiss deepened, his tongue finding its way into my mouth, tasting me, exploring me.

I jumped about a foot in the air when I heard Bridgette's voice shouting, "Oh, my God!" My head whipped around, facing her.

"I'm sorry... I had no idea... erm... the door was open, and I just needed to ask you where you buy those little pastel butter mints from—"

My hand went to my mouth, wiping at my smudged lipstick. "Uh, no, its fine. We were just..."

"Sucking face?" Bridgette answered helpfully, a smirk on her face.

I looked to Hayes. He was not amused. "Bridgette—you need something?" he asked, walking over to where she stood.

"Yeah—like I said, the mints. Hey, are you guys like official, now—" Hayes had Bridgette firmly by the upper arm and was guiding her right out the door, her blonde curls bouncing as she went.

Hayes said, "She'll find them for you. Bye, Bridgette."

Bridgette peeked over her shoulder at me, mouthing 'text me' as Hayes pushed her out the door. Closing the door behind her, Hayes' smoldering eyes locked on mine, asking, "Where were we?"

Suddenly shy, I smiled, looking down at my shoes. We were in my office, during a workday... but why not? I had always done the right thing and look where that had gotten me... lonely. I spent one night doing the wrong thing and it had resulted in me having amazing orgasms.

Biting my bottom lip, I reached for the hem of my shirt, pulling it up and over my bra. I tossed the shirt on the desk, eyeing Hayes and beckoning him to come closer.

Giving me a sexy grin, he twisted the lock on the doorknob. "Come to Daddy," he said. The words sent a thrill though me.

He strode toward me. Goosebumps rose on my flesh at his nearness. His hands wrapped around the bare skin of my back. His fingers walked up my spine, reaching the clasp of my bra. Snapping it open, he removed my bra, freeing my breasts. Stepping back, his eyes took me in, the grin spreading on his face. "You are a beauty, Louanne. A work of art." Eyes locked on mine, he began to unbutton his shirt. I watched as the smooth tanned skin of his chest was slowly exposed.

Placing his shirt on the desk, he wrapped his arms around me, holding me against his chest. My bare breasts pressed against him, my nipples hardening. His mouth went to my earlobe, nibbling and sucking. He whispered in my ear, "I can spoil you when you're good," his hand went to my ass, grabbing it tightly, "spank you when you are bad," his fingers walked their way around my hip, slipping down the front of my pants, "pet your little pussy till—"

I jumped out of my skin at the sound of the door opening again.

"Oh, my God! I'm sorry! Why the hell wasn't this door

locked? Don't you guys know how to lock a door!" I peeked over Hayes' shoulder to see Georgia. Her pale skin was flushed, her cheeks red. Her green eyes were wide, her mouth open to continue her explanation.

Hayes' head lolled back, exasperation etched in his face. "Leave now, Georgia. And close the door behind you."

Georgia continued to mutter her string of apologies on her way out, closing the door behind her.

"Those girls are in so much trouble," Hayes said, running his fingers through his hair.

"Why? We were the ones kissing at work. And it totally slipped my mind that the lock on my office door is funky— you have to turn it all the way around and hear it click to be sure it's locked—but I've never needed it before."

Hayes raised a brow to me. "You mean to tell me you think it was a coincidence that Bridgette and Georgia both visited your office this morning?"

I shrugged. "Well, Bridgette needed the mints and Georgia—"

"Bridgette does not need mints. She just saw you come in this morning, got nosy, and wanted to see if I was in here with you. Then, she saw us kissing, went straight to Georgia. Georgia wanted to see it for herself, then came busting in here. They had best hope I don't tell my brothers on them," he said.

I thought about Hayes' theory. As much as I loved those two girls, I couldn't defend them. It was likely what he said was true.

I sighed, moving toward him. "Nosy girls. We have really got to find them both a hobby."

Hayes wrapped his arms back around me, kissing my cheek. "Their hobby is going to be standing in the corner with smacked bottoms if they don't stay out of this office." His lips went to my neck, sucking and kissing. "Where were we?"

Finally, my good girl took a break and let my bad girl have the office sex she had been craving—right on top of my perfectly polished desk. It was amazing. I didn't want to risk going back to the Louanne who didn't take chances, who was always the good girl. Being that way had delayed my getting together with Hayes, and I didn't want to move backwards.

How could I keep that from happening?

I would write myself a list. A list of reasons why I needed to loosen up and let life happen. Better yet, a letter—a reminder of all the times I didn't take a chance and should have. I plopped my notebook down on my christened desk and wrote a letter to myself.

*Dear Louanne,*

*Please, please, please don't mess this up! For the first time in over two years your body has gone from being a retired old bag of bones with cobwebs forming between your legs, to a marvelous palace of pleasure.*

*Do not mess this up with Hayes.*

*It's time for old Louanne to loosen up and let her hair down. To embrace the daddy/baby girl way of life and live outside the good girl box.*

*Let it be known, yes, your Type A, nose to the grindstone personality is no doubt the reason for your success, but it has often gotten in the way of having fun! Too often, you say 'no' when you should be saying 'yes.' And that stops now, because finally saying 'yes' to dating Hayes has been the best decision of your life.*

*Here are some reminders of times you said 'no' and should have said 'yes.' For example, when Bridgette and Georgia were going to the Male Review for Georgia's bachelorette party and didn't go because you wanted to finish up tying personalized M&M's in those little netted baggies, you missed out! Although after seeing the tanned, muscular chest of Hayes Jenkins, you had more than made up for what you didn't see that night on the Chip and Dale stage. And they both got in super big trouble when Brody found out. And you would have probably hated the experience anyway—sweaty half naked strangers rubbing their neon green thong banana hammocks on your thigh… yuck.*

*Bad example.*

*What about when Josie wanted you to go to that concert in Jackson*

Hole but you stayed behind because the pygmy goats were being delivered for the yoga retreat and you wanted to make sure they were comfortable? The drummer thought Josie was cute and brought all the girls backstage to meet the band. Josie got her bra signed by the lead guitarist and six months later the band was so big she was able to sell her 32B cup for three hundred dollars. Oh, but getting a few extra hours holding those precious little animals was priceless! And Hayes had just come back on the ranch as your boss. He knew you had passed up the concert to work and so he took you to the diner, just the two of you, you ate hamburgers and fries and spent three hours in the same booth catching up one another's lives. It was the best evening. So, also not a good example.

What about the time that cute doctor at the rainbow-themed wedding asked you out? He was nice and polite. His mother was an excellent dancer. At the time you hadn't had a date in well over a year. During the reception, you got to talking and found that you were both allergic to polyester. You joked about it for a while—he had been easy enough to talk to. Then, one of the guests fell, skinning their knees. You brought him the first aid kit and helped him patch up the injured party. Afterwards, he asked you for a drink. You froze, holding the gauze in your sweaty palm, your mouth going dry. Then, you said you were busy. Too busy for a drink, he had joked. The next day, you had regretted not saying yes. But a few months later, Hayes came back. And the rest is history. What if you had said yes to that drink? And the doctor and you had hit it off? Hayes would never have shown you interest if you had been spoken for—he may not have even come back to the ranch! Oh, dear, that would have been terrible—you might have missed getting together with Hayes, your soulmate, had you said yes to the doctor! So… another terrible example.

Well, this letter has completely backfired from its original purpose. If anything, it is a reminder to just go with my heart and say yes to what feels right.

Signing off,

Type A, workaholic, perfectionist to a 't,' perfectly happy being the good girl (except with Hayes) Louanne

# CHAPTER FOUR

The following weeks went by in a happy bliss. So happy, I almost forgot that *Travel and Dining*'s lead editor, Eloise Smarts, was coming to interview us for the spread. It was the day before they were due to arrive when I remembered our appointment. I stayed up till well past midnight, making the final preparations for their visit.

When they arrived at the Mess Hall via the CLAS minibus, nerves fluttered in my stomach at the number of people present. The last person to exit the bus was a short woman dressed head to toe in a white linen pantsuit. After the long ride from the airport to the ranch, she did not have a single wrinkle on her clothing—which is incredibly impressive to anyone who has ever worked with linen. She marched right over to me and began talking. "*Travel and Dining*'s Top Ten is quite an honor. We do hope you understand that, Miss Louanne." Eloise peered at me over the rim of her purple-framed glasses. Her hand delicately fluttered to her short red bulletproof hair.

Nervously, I rambled, "I certainly do, Eloise. I was speechless when I first heard that CLAS had made the list. Just speechless. Brody took the team out to dinner, then at the very end of the meal, he announced we had made the list! Here I was just doing my best creating simple but beautiful weddings for our clients—"

She held up a perfectly manicured hand to stop me. "Drop the word 'simple' right now. There is nothing simple about what you do here. I mean, the views are breathtaking—and not just the mountains—and the staff is gorgeous, but it's all quite rustic. To bring in elegance and charm to a ranch—well, it's a miracle really."

I couldn't tell if CLAS had been complimented or insulted. Though it was clear that she found our cowboys easy on the eyes. "Thank you?" I replied.

During their visit, I spent the entire day with Eloise and her team of photographers. We tromped over every inch of the ranch. They took pictures of the guest cabins. Georgia and Bridgette had spent an entire week making sure each room was neat as a pin. Memaw's kitchen was spotless and they got an adorable photo of her standing by her commercial stove wearing her red-checked apron, wooden spoon in hand.

Josie had done up the Mess Hall with our Pink and White Fairy Princess décor I had chosen for the shoot, knowing it would look the best on the glossy pages of the magazine. Colton showed them around the activities we offered families during their stay. The boating, fishing, and horseback riding would all make it into the article. And of course, the barn.

Eloise gasped with delight when she entered the barn. I had gone with 'Romantic Ranch' and doubled the number of LED candles and white roses—this time, fresh ones. I had spared no expense, knowing the investment would come back to us two-fold with new clients.

After the full tour and a meal of Memaw's home cooking, Eloise asked if we could sit in my office for a private interview with 'America's Best Wedding Planner.' (Her words, not mine!)

Eloise pulled a giant notebook from her massive purse. The bag had a woven tapestry look to it and reminded me of Mary Poppins' bottomless carpetbag. "We've spent the day together, but I'd like to get to know you better. Delve into the psyche that is Louanne Dixon. Such a... quaint name." She gave me a hard stare over her glasses.

Again, compliment or insult? I snuck a peek at my clock on the wall, holding in a sigh. I was exhausted from the prep work for this day, as well as by the tour. I was ready to bid our guest farewell and crawl under my giant heap of fluffy comforters.

She turned to a blank page in her notebook. "Now, tell me about your signature cocktail."

"I don't have one," I shrugged.

Her eyes widened. "What? Every great wedding planner must have a signature cocktail. Now don't be coy—what is yours?"

"I have a delicious sorbet punch. A minty mock Mojito. Oh, and everyone's favorite, my raspberry and mint tea. Before I pour the tea over the ice, I add a few frozen raspberries and mint leaves to the glass. The trick is to freeze the mint leaves, too. Any garnish in a cold drink holds up so much better when frozen."

She jotted a few notes down, murmuring, "And what is the tea spiked with? Rum?"

I gave a chuckle at the idea of rum at one of our weddings. Brody would have a heart attack—or take whoever had brought the hard liquor onto his ranch right over his knee for a sound spanking—if there was rum. "There is no alcohol allowed on the premises. The owner is a staunch teetotaler. Straight edge. Clean as a whistle and as dry as a desert. Hence the name of the ranch—Clean Living and Sunshine."

She gasped in horror. "No alcohol? Then how do your guests have a good time?"

I answered, "We've actually been told that our weddings are better for the family members of the bride and groom— no alcohol, no drama. Without the intoxication, ex-girlfriends no longer feel the need to approach the groom and give one last plea at a reconciliation. Your aunt Glenda isn't feeling quite as brave and refrains from telling you she thinks you're a floozy for living with your husband before marriage and that your dress should be cream, not white. And the speeches from the fathers are much more... touching. Without inebriation, humiliating stories about embarrassing thing you did when you were six years old don't seem to come up as often."

"Ah—so, you've been a bride? Experienced these things firsthand for yourself? Sounds like quite a family you have yourself there, Louanne," she laughed.

I held up my left hand, signaling to the bare ring finger. "Nope. Just word of mouth from our guests."

Eloise placed a hand on her chest, drawing back in shock. "You mean to tell me you're not... married? However do you pull off such beautiful events without being able to tap into your inner bride?"

I shrugged. "Pinterest? My imagination? Lots and lots of lists?"

Eloise leaned in, whispering as if she were telling me her darkest secret while seated in a room full of people. "But please, tell me you aren't... *single*? Not with all these handsome, muscular men roaming around? They all look quite... capable."

"I was single, actually. For years. I've only recently become attached. And yes, I'm a lucky girl. I happened to be with one of our, as you put it, capable, men," I said.

Her eyes lit up. She asked in a hushed whisper, "Which one?"

"Hayes—he's the one with lighter hair and the blue eyes—"

She smiled. "Oh, those blue-gray eyes? He's the most handsome for sure. You are a lucky girl, aren't you? Are you two thinking of tying the knot?"

Hayes had practically proposed marriage within twenty-four hours of our first kiss. But getting married hadn't really crossed my mind yet. Even though we'd known one another for years, our relationship was still new. "Well, now... I, ah... I don't know. It's kind of fresh—"

She interrupted me by clapping her hands together. "You know what would be lovely for the magazine? Just lovely?"

"No... I, ah—"

Excitement rose in her voice. She spoke quickly, her hands clasped before her. "If you and Hayes were to marry, *Travel and Dining* could cover not just any wedding, but *your* wedding. *The wedding of the wedding planner!* Can you imagine how many readers would pick up a copy of our magazine to read your article!"

"We aren't even engaged," I said.

"I've seen the way he looks at you—trust me, it can't be far off. My second husband looked at me that very same way and we were engaged after only dating two months. Now my third husband on the other hand... I should have known that wasn't going to work out—"

Feeling a bit overwhelmed, I said, "Eloise, I think it would be best if we just did the article as planned."

For the first time since she arrived in my office, Eloise got quiet. She leaned in even further than before. "Is it the money? They would pay you quite handsomely, you know. For the rights to the story."

"What *story*?" I asked. Frustration began to creep in over my fatigue.

"The wedding planner that finally gets her own dream wedding. Can you imagine the photos? And you—with that perfectly milky skin and rosebud mouth. We might even be able to get you on the cover. Can you imagine the photoshoot? We are talking Vera Wang here. We could get a professional hair and makeup team flown in to do you up gorgeous. I'm sure Eddie will let me put you on the cover. He owes me a favor after I kept quiet about that misprint last month. And the gowns! Oh, the gowns. Vera will be so pleased to know one of our Top Ten is wearing her designs."

Vera Wang? Designer wedding gowns? Professional hair and makeup? Being photographed for the cover of a magazine? And not to mention the money. Hayes and I could afford a white sand beach vacation. It was tempting. After all, Hayes had kind of sort of already proposed...

Eloise saw me cracking. Placing a soft hand over mine, she said, "Tell you what. You think about it, Louanne. We will focus on this spread—get ready for the Top Ten to go out. Then, just before it goes to print, you let me know if we can attach a sort of 'stay tuned' block in there with a photo of you and Hayes announcing the engagement and letting the readers know the coverage of the wedding is coming up in a special edition. Just think about it."

I couldn't believe it when the question slipped from my lips. "How long until the magazine goes to print?"

A light shone in her face. "Eight weeks. You have eight weeks to become engaged to that hunk of a man." She gave me a wink.

I could already feel the Alencon lace brushing against my 'perfectly milky' skin.

After Eloise left my office, I sat at my desk, considering her proposal. I was not ready to be married. Engaged, perhaps. I couldn't deny I had tried on a few giant cubic zirconia rings the last time I was puttering around Target. But married—was I even old enough to be wed?

And the wife of a strict daddy? That was a whole 'nother commitment in and of itself.

But to be featured in a magazine, head to toe styled in Vera Wang? Professional hair and makeup? That was a once in a lifetime opportunity.

I was ready for the photoshoot, the beautiful dresses, the hair and makeup. I just wasn't ready for the marriage part.

How could I have my three-tiered vanilla buttercream wedding cake and eat it too? What about a fake engagement? I just had to get Hayes to agree to go along with it. It was too soon for the real thing, but if we just told a little white lie and let Eloise think that we were engaged, I could do the article. Could I get my daddy to agree to the plan? Maybe with a little sweet talking.

I thought over the idea. I had a feeling Daddy was not going to like it. Little knots formed in my stomach at the thought of his eyes turning gray and flashing at me disapprovingly. I didn't have the nerve to face him. I would leave him a note. Who am I kidding... I would leave him a list. They'd always worked for me in the past!

Carefully, I pulled a sheet of paper from my notebook and got my favorite pen out of my desk drawer. I began writing.

*Dearest Hayes,*

*I have a teeny, tiny favor to ask of you. Eloise from Travel and Dining would love to do a spread about me. She said it would pay handsomely, and I would get to play bride. A team would come out and doll me up in wedding finery and they'd put my picture on the cover. What wedding planner doesn't have a lifelong dream of getting to wear a Vera Wang gown? The only catch is that the photoshoot would be linked to an article about us getting married. It's way too soon for that, but this is an opportunity I just can't pass up. I am proposing we fake the engagement and I do the photoshoot. Now, I know you probably won't like this idea, so I've made a little list for you to think over. Love you!*

*Louanne*

*Perfectly Good Reasons to Fake Our Engagement*
1. *Vera Wang*
2. *Makeup*
3. *Hair*
4. *Being on the cover of a magazine!*
5. *The money*
6. *Once in a lifetime opportunity*
7. *Great for the ranch's business*
8. *Will bring in new clients for CLAS*
9. *Practice for being engaged one day down the road*
10. *Working with Eloise again—she is awesome*

11. *Getting a second article in T & D (I still can't believe we got the first one!)*
12. *The article about us might bump CLAS's number up in the T & D's Top Ten for next year*
13. *It's not super dishonest because we love each other, right? It's just a teeny, tiny white lie.*
14. *Right?*

I chewed on the end of my pen as I read over the list. My arguments were weak at best. But I had to give it a go. Who knew... maybe Hayes would surprise me and say 'yes.' Leaving my office, paper in hand, I tromped over the ranch looking for Hayes.

I found him in the back of the Mess Hall, tightening the legs of the benches. We had so many guests in and out these days, Hayes had taken to checking the nuts and bolts on the benches and tables weekly. He smiled brightly when he saw me approach, calling, "Hey, baby girl!"

Rushing over to him, I melted into his arms, murmuring, "Hey, yourself, Daddy."

His lips met mine, causing a warm liquid feeling to flow through my body. I drank up the endorphins as we kissed, my head feeling fuzzy.

He pulled away too soon, untangling me from his torso. He pulled the crumpled paper from my hands. "What's this?" he asked, gazing over my scribbled words.

"It's, ah... a list," I said, flashing what I hoped was a dazzling smile.

He read over the note. His brow knitted as he murmured, "Perfectly good reasons to fake our engagement?" His eyes flashed up to me once, then his gaze went back to the paper.

My shoulders tensed as I watched him read. I was beginning to think this was a really bad idea. I clasped my hands behind me, waiting for him to finish. As he continued to read, the little muscle in his jaw started twitching.

When he was finished, he handed the paper back to me.

I pasted on a fake smile, saying brightly, "So, what do you think?"

"Absolutely not. And I should take you over my knee for suggesting such a thing," he growled, running a hand through his sandy hair. "What were you thinking when you wrote this?"

A little shiver ran through me at his threat. I stammered, "I... uh... I honestly I was only thinking of trying on those gorgeous dresses."

His gray eyes flashed with anger. "Lying to a magazine? Faking the most important commitment you will make in your lifetime? Is that what marriage is to you? A joke?"

I knew Hayes wouldn't like the idea, per se, but I hadn't anticipated him being this against it. "It's just for fun, Daddy. It sounded so princess-like. Getting to have professionals doll you up for the day. Having photographers take your picture in a designer gown. Be on the cover of a magazine. Nearly the past decade of my life has been all about weddings. It makes sense that I would want to get to participate in the glam side of things. Doesn't it?" I asked.

His firm daddy tone came out. His hands went to his hips as he towered over me. "You'd be participating in dishonesty. And dragging me into the lie with you. That's naughty, Louanne. And if you don't see how wrong it is then you need a little trip over my knee to open your eyes. I just finished tightening the legs on this bench. I'd be more than happy to test it out by sitting right down and—"

"I'm sorry! You're right. It was a terrible idea," I said, my hands going to my bottom.

He eyed me, unconvinced.

That sinking feeling started welling in my stomach. The pulsing of my pussy wet my panties. My body was confusing me with its sexy/scared reactions. Wasn't that always the way when you were in trouble and knew you were about to be spanked?

I began to back away from Hayes. I stammered, "I-I'm going to get back to work. Please, just forget I even suggested it. It was a terrible idea."

Hayes took a step toward me. I began to perspire.

"What kind of daddy would I be if I didn't spank my little girl when she proposed such a naughty scheme?"

"The forgiving type? Everyone makes mistakes," I said.

His big hand wrapped around my arm. Seconds later, he was seated on the bench, and I was over his lap. He had done a lovely job on the bench legs—it hadn't even wobbled when he sat down. "I can't let this one go, baby girl. Just reading that note made me... so angry."

"It was meant as a means to an end. I just really wanted the opportunity. I promise, I didn't mean any harm!" My protests were useless as my skirt was being lifted up and over my bottom. To add to my shame, he tucked the hem of my skirt into its waistband to keep it in place. I had a feeling we were going to be here awhile.

The cool air sent goosebumps down my thighs as I prayed to the heavens above not to let anyone walk into the Mess Hall and see me laying over Daddy's lap, my white panties on display. I squeezed my eyes shut tightly as his hand rested on my waiting bottom.

"Marriage is a sacred bond between two people and should not be made into a joke, young lady. It concerns me how lightly you take that vow—especially considering your career choice." His hand lightly patted my bottom. Tingles ran from my bottom to my pussy. My buttocks clenched, my pussy tightened as I waited for him to spank me.

He gave my ass a light slap. The sound was loud in the hall, though the spank only stung slightly. "Tell Daddy how sorry you are for wanting to make up a lie."

"I-I'm very sorry, Daddy. It won't happen again." Butterflies tickled my tummy. The balls of my feet pressed into the floor. Was he going to spank me lightly again? It felt so good. Being over his lap and having him chastise me like a naughty little girl while spanking me over my panties was turning me on. My nipples tightened against my bra. My pussy wept and pulsed, wanting to be wrapped around his cock. He spanked me again, on the middle of my bottom. Despite my best efforts to stay still, my hips wiggled. As they did, my clit was pushed against my slick folds, which dug into his muscular hip. I could feel a hard bulge forming in his jeans, his cock hardening against my stomach.

"Oh, Daddy, please don't spank me anymore. I'll be such a good girl, I promise!" I cried.

"Daddy's not done with you yet, little one. You haven't learned your lesson. Do you need to stand in the corner of this Mess Hall? I'll leave your skirt up just like this and everyone can come in and admire you in your pretty white panties. They'll know you were a naughty girl and that your loving daddy took the time to properly punish you. What do you think?" Another delicious stinging spank landed on my bottom.

"Oh, no, Daddy! Only you can see me in my panties! Please don't make me stand in the corner," I cried.

"Well, if you don't want anyone to see your panties, maybe I should take them off." His fingertips slid into the waistband of my panties. He pulled them down until my bottom was bared. "It would be best to spank this pretty little bottom on the bare, first. Then, when you are in the corner, everyone will see how red Daddy made your ass."

"No, Daddy, no! Please don't spank my bare bottom," I protested. I buried my face in my hands as a shameful grin spread over my face.

His hand came down, a loud 'smack' echoed through the hall. He spanked my bare bottom, alternating between hard and light smacks. My skin was becoming warmer with each spank. Tingles danced over my bottom. My pussy was hot and melty. I squeezed my legs together and moved my hips, massaging my clit against his thigh and giving myself pleasure. I had never been so turned on. "I only wanted to look pretty in the magazine, Daddy. Please don't spank me," I cried while in my mind, I begged, *please don't stop spanking me!*

"I want you to be able to do the magazine, sweetheart."

His hand rested on my warm bottom. "I only want you to do it honestly."

My hips stopped moving. I turned my head over my shoulder, trying to see his face. I asked, "What are you proposing?"

He pulled my panties up over my bottom. Carefully, he removed the hem of my skirt from my waistband and laid it back down over my bottom. He helped me up from over his legs and sat me on his lap. His arms wrapped protectively around me. His hand went to the side of my face. Those blue-gray eyes locked on mine. He said, "Marry me."

I froze. His words hung in the air before me. Heat crept up my neck. My heart had trouble finding its rhythm. "I... I... I can't. We are too young and have only been dating a few weeks and I'd make a terrible wife—you know how bossy I am and—"

His brow furrowed. His jaw clenched. He got that look he gets before I get into big trouble. "Louanne, are you saying no to marrying me now, or ever? Because I don't date without the intention of the relationship going somewhere. If this isn't going anywhere, you need to tell me now."

"What? I'm head over heels in love with you, Hayes! What are you talking about?" I asked.

"I am asking you if you see yourself marrying me or not." His eyes flashed with concern.

"Are you giving me an ultimatum? Marry you, or break up?" I gasped.

"No. I'm simply asking you to ask yourself what your intentions are," he said.

What were my intentions? I stammered, "I-I love you, Hayes. Isn't that enough?"

When he spoke, his words sent a shiver down my spine. Goosebumps rose along my arms. "I love you too, Luna. But I want more than that. Because one day, down the road, after a big fight or a long day, we might not be feeling that love. And until that feeling comes back, I want to know that we made a vow—that we committed ourselves to one another. In good times, and in bad. Marriage is a pact you make with another person that goes beyond love."

Tears sprang up in my eyes. I had never heard marriage described so beautifully in my entire life—and I had been around a lot of weddings. I threw my arms around Hayes' neck, burying my face in his chest. "You're right, Hayes. And I do want to... marry you."

He pulled me from him, holding my shoulders. He leaned down, his intense stare studying my gaze. "You mean it, Luna?"

I nodded, brushing at the tears that threatened to fall. A huge smile spread across his face. He grabbed me up underneath my arms and stood up, lifted me into the air. I laughed as he spun me around in a circle, yelling, "Yeehaw!" When he finally put me down, I was dizzy, and he had to hold my arms to steady me.

"Let's do this properly." Hayes sat me down on the bench. Then, he got down on one knee before me. "Louanne Dixon, will you be my wife?"

"Yes," I answered, still laughing from his excitement.

My eyes widened as I watched Hayes pull a small black velvet box from his pocket. My hands went to my mouth, covering up my gasp as he opened the little lid with a soft 'click.' My heart fluttered at the sight of what was inside the box. A gorgeous ring. The sparkling oval-shaped center diamond looked to be at least two carats and it was framed by a halo of set side stones to add further lavishness to the design. The ring's shank was also adorned with a triple row of tiny diamonds. It was the most beautiful thing I had ever seen.

I gasped. "Where did you get that... have you just been carrying it around with you? Oh, my goodness, Hayes. It's beautiful."

He took my left hand in his. Taking the ring from the box, he slipped it onto my ring finger. I held my hand out, watching the diamond sparkle as I turned my finger this way and that under the lights of the Mess Hall. It was gorgeous.

Hayes stood up, wrapping his arm around my shoulders. "It's been in my pocket since the day after our first kiss. A man just never knows when he's going to need to propose."

It was the most romantic thing I'd heard of. I threw my arms around him and kissed my fiancé.

And in one magical moment I went from wedding planner to bride to be.

• • • • • • •

The phone call to Eloise was almost as exciting as telling my sister I was getting married. Josie hopped up and down clapping and begging to be my maid of honor. Eloise shrieked into the phone then began jabbering and planning the multitude of possible poses I could show off potential dresses in. Both women were equally excited.

We told my mother and Alice, Hayes' mom, together. They cried and hugged one another, both proclaiming they knew this day would come. Then we shared the news with the rest of the ranch at a congratulatory dinner Memaw cooked for us.

Just when the excitement and buzz about the engagement began to die down around the ranch, Eloise sent out *Travel and Dining*'s photography team. They were followed by a gaggle of over-made-up women who each had about a can of spray in their hair and lipstick that was two shades too dark. But the dresses they brought with them forgave any makeup mistakes they had made.

My goodness, those dresses.

I had longed to put one of those gorgeous, perfect, pure white dresses on my body since I was twelve years old. I got my first subscription to *Brides* at the age of fifteen. As a teen, when my friends were out partying with the football team, I sat on my bed, doodling designs for wedding gowns. And now, I was finally getting to wear one.

And not just any chain store bridal gown—though I would have been quite happy with that option had this amazing opportunity not presented itself. These dresses were handmade, one of a kind with designer's names proudly emblazed over the tags.

The one I cherished most was the hand-beaded sparkling sweetheart neckline with the lace-capped sleeves. When the makeup artist unzipped that baby blue garment bag, I knew it was the one, even before the words 'Vera Wang' crossed her lips.

Knowing I would soon be wearing that dress, I barely felt the women pulling and tugging at my pin-straight hair as they tried to tease and spray it into submission. "Go light on the makeup. She's a natural beauty," the lady in the burgundy lipstick said, smiling at me as she lightly stroked powder on my face. When they were done with me, the woman stood back, admiring their handiwork. Then, they slipped me into the Vera Wang.

Standing before the mirror, tears sprang in my eyes as I twirled. The heavy fabric fell into place so beautifully, I felt as if I were on the set of a movie. The beadwork glimmered and sparkled beneath the lights. I couldn't take my eyes off the intricate details.

"It's perfect."

"She's perfect."

"That dress looks like it was made for her."

"Maybe it was. I always thought Vera might be a fairy godmother in disguise."

I smiled shyly at their compliments. I felt like the most beautiful girl in the world. And it was time to take my picture. Encapsulate the fleeting moment that would soon be over.

Modeling for a magazine is a lot harder work than it looks. You have to contort your body into all kinds of uncomfortable positions, then tilt your head just so and place your hands in the right location. Then, hold the pose until the cameraman gets the lighting the way he wants it and takes the photo. But with that cool silk against my skin and the weight of the dress pressed against me, I didn't care.

When it was over, Memaw happily fed the crowd, eager to have them gone. People tended to leave quicker when they were full, ready to have a rest in the bus on the ride back to the airport. Brody had offered them all cabins to stay the night, but they had another shoot in the morning and had to be off.

As the photographer was leaving, he called out to me, "Don't forget to send Eloise the details for your wedding. She can't wait!"

A ball of ice formed in my stomach, all the excitement of the photoshoot melting away with his words. I realized I hadn't yet made a single plan for my own wedding.

As soon as the bus pulled away with the team, I hurried to my office and pulled out my notebook. I needed to make a list. As I sat there, my eyelids started to droop. There was not a word on my paper when Hayes came and took me by the arm, leading me to the truck. He drove me home and tucked me into bed. Before he left, he kissed my forehead and said, "Sweet dreams, baby girl. There will never be a more beautiful bride than you."

Drifting off to sleep, I smiled, dreaming of lace and silk.

# CHAPTER FIVE

Memaw's face popped out from behind the Mess Hall kitchen door. "Louanne, call for you! Get in here, honey. The way this fella is breathing into the phone sounds like he's gonna have a heart attack if you keep him waiting much longer!" The door swung shut and she disappeared.

Georgia looked at me curiously. "Who could that be? I assumed everyone who needed to call you has your direct line."

I shrugged, wiping my hands on my napkin. "Once in a while we get a call from someone who found our number in the phone book. The ranch kitchen is listed as our main number."

Bridgette scrunched up her nose, helping herself to another piece of garlic bread. "What's a phone book?"

"It's like the internet but with yellow pages. Brody insisted we list our number in there. It's the only way people could contact him back in the Stone Age when he opened this place and there was no such thing as cell phones." I sighed, standing from my bench. I hated to leave behind Memaw's baked spaghetti, but lunch would have to wait.

I hurried into the kitchen, brushing past Memaw as she grumbled, "Took you long enough," and picked up the phone receiver from the counter. Stretching its cord to its maximum length, I tried to find a quieter corner of the room.

"Hello? Louanne Dixon speaking," I said, leaning against the wall and twirling the cord around my hand.

A heavy breathing came through the other line. In between heaves, a blunt voice demanded, "Is this the wedding planner?"

My nose wrinkling, I answered, "Uh... yes. This is she."

"Brian. Brian O'Malley. Pleasure to," his introduction was cut off by a coughing fit, "make your acquaintance. I'm a reporter from the *Little Peak Times*. We've gotten word that you have quite the wedding operation going out up there at the ranch."

"Yes, sir. Thank you. We feel that marriage is the—"

"I'll stop you right there, little missy. I was married for thirty years to the love of my life. God rest her soul. I've been a bachelor for ten and I'm perfectly happy—I've no need for your services. The real reason I'm calling is the Top Ten," he said.

"Oh, so you've heard we made the list?" I asked, trying to sound surprised. The day the *T & D* article on the ranch hit, everyone in Little Peak had called to congratulate us. Memaw threatened to take the phone off the hook if the calls didn't slow down.

The article doubled as an engagement announcement. At the end of the spread there was a small information box with a pretty floral border. Within it were the words, *Wedding planner extraordinaire, Louanne Dixon and her groom, Hayes Jenkins are planning their own wedding. It's sure to top all others. Stay tuned with* Travel and Dining *for a special release covering the lovebirds' nuptials.*

That Sunday, the Little Peak Baptist Woman's Guild threw us a surprise shower after church, making our engagement feel official. I was told, more than once, "We've been waiting for this day since you two were in high school!"

Brian spoke loudly. "Yes, of course I heard you made

the list!" His excitement caused his breath to quicken. "Who hasn't? I think the news made it all the way to Jackson. Anyhow, I'd love to come do an interview with you for the paper about your wedding planning business. How about two p.m.?" he wheezed.

My brows rose in surprise. "Two o'clock, as in two o'clock today?" At four o' clock I was meeting with a family who was considering throwing a sweet sixteen ball at the ranch, and I had blocked off the entire afternoon to prepare.

"Yes, today. We've got to hit this news while it's still fresh. Trust me, the people of Little Peak are salt of the Earth—but they have an extremely short attention span. What do you say, Louanne? After your taste of fame with *T & D*, don't you want to see your name in print again?" he asked.

"I mean, I don't care about my name in print, but I'd hate to pass up an opportunity for the ranch—"

"Two o'clock it is! See you then." He hung up the phone so quickly I wasn't sure if he was trying to avoid giving me time to change my mind, or if he needed to go find an inhaler or something. Memaw hadn't been exaggerating about the man's breathing.

At two o'clock on the dot, there was a knock on my office door. Standing and smoothing my skirt, I called, "Come in."

The door opened and a stout man in a tweed suit let himself into the room. His suit jacket was buttoned, the material straining around his barrel-like torso. He took a few deep breaths, then grabbed my hand. His palm was sweaty as he pumped my arm up and down. "Louanne Dixon, you're as pretty as a picture. Brian O'Malley. A pleasure to meet you in person." He plopped himself down on one of my buffalo-checked club chairs, throwing a notebook on the table.

I was surprised by how much I instantly liked the strange man. Taking a seat, I smiled. "So nice to have you here today. My mother and I read the *Times* every Sunday."

"The *New York Times?* Good for you," he laughed.

"No, of course, the *Little Peak Times*. It's charming and we enjoy keeping up with the happenings in our community."

"Well, I appreciate it. We are a small paper but have been fortunate in the fact that Little Peak seems to be a place where time stands still. When internet papers came around, many other small-time presses came to a close, but the inhabitants of our town still like to hold that paper in their hands. Nothing like a cup of coffee and black ink smudges on your fingers while reading a good story," he said.

"I couldn't agree more." I didn't add that my sister loved that ink when she was a girl and stuck every kind of Play-Doh and putty to the paper, watching the ink from the black words magically transfer from the pages.

Pulling a pair of horn-rimmed glasses from his breast pocket, he unfolded the metal frame, balancing them on the bridge of his nose. He pulled a pen from the same pocket, then peered at me over the glasses. "Miss Louanne, if you don't mind, I'll get right down to the questioning. How many weddings do you host per year?"

"I plan and host events on the ranch every weekend, but weddings I keep to one a month—two at max if there is an emergency. I like to be sure to give the bride the attention that she deserves and that just isn't possible if you are dealing with more than two brides at a time."

His bushy eyebrows rose as he said, "Emergency?"

"Yes. Emergency as in one year I had already committed to an April wedding, but then this poor dear called me telling me her father was going to have surgery in May and there was no way he would be able to walk her down the aisle until after summer and she so had her heart set on a spring wedding. I managed to add her to the month. It was a busy one—I don't think I sat down to dinner once, last April."

"Couldn't she just have gotten married the following spring? What's the big deal?" he asked.

I held in a laugh. "That would be... unacceptable."

He eyed me. "How so?"

There were two people in this world. People who understood brides. And people who didn't. It appeared that Mr. O'Malley fell into the latter category. "Unacceptable to wait another year. If the engagement goes on too long, the bride irrationally begins to fear the groom will lose interest before the knot is tied. Or, that she will go crazy if wedding plans drag on another minute, much less another year. Or, she just can't hear one more person rob her joy by telling her that she is too young to wed, or her groom's ears stick out too far and does she want children with that problem as well, or that they will not be buying a gift off of her registry but instead will be giving her homemade potholders," I heaved a Brian O'Malley-like breath and sat back in my chair. "I've seen it all."

"Potholders, huh? Go figure. I'd think a dame would love a good set of potholders," he shrugged, jotting down the word 'potholders' on his paper. "How many weddings have you done, total, Miss Louanne?"

"This next wedding will be my one hundred and twenty-fifth wedding," I said.

His jaw dropped open.

"I only did a handful of those the first few years, but then the business really picked up," I said.

"How do you keep up with it all? I mean, not only do you have the weddings, you have the other events, too." He looked at me as if expecting an equation for building a rocket ship.

I shrugged. "Lists."

"Lists?" he asked doubtfully.

"Lists," I said. Standing, I walked over the long black file drawers that lined one wall of my office. I pulled out a drawer, revealing rows and rows of neatly marked file folders. They all held lists. Mr. O'Malley stood from his chair, plodding over to join me. "Each folder holds a bride—well, not a bride, a wedding. And within that folder is each and every list that I made for her special occasion. As I'm planning the wedding, I keep the current lists in a notebook in my bag—I take it everywhere with me, you never know when a list is going to hit you—then when the happy day is successful and over, I file them away here. I have a file for every event I've hosted as well. Those grew so large, Hayes had to move them into boxes and store them in one of the sheds on the property."

"This is… unreal," he said, his gaze roving over the drawer.

"Thank you," I answered primly. "I pride myself on my organization."

"So… uh… what's a lady like you do for fun?" he asked.

Was he mocking me?

"This *is* fun." Had the man never had the satisfaction of ticking off a box at the end of the day? Or organizing his chaotic ideas into neatly numbered rows? There was nothing like it in this world.

"Fun… huh? You're so young though. Don't you do stuff other than work?" he asked.

"Yes. I go to the salon. I take my mother to lunch. Oh— the other day I went to Bud's with the girls for the first time," I said in my defense.

His brow rose. "Bud's is the only bar in town and you are just now making it down there for a drink?"

"I think working is fun," I said.

"Sounds like a lot on your plate though. Can one person manage both events and weddings?" he said doubtfully.

"I have part-time help. I'm fine," I protested.

"How many hours do you work in a week?" he asked.

"Is this a question for the interview?" I asked.

"No, I'm just curious how one person gets all this done. Are you like a robot or something?" He peeked behind my back as if looking for a control panel.

"Mr. O'Malley. I am a very busy woman… as you have already ascertained. Let's sit down and finish this interview, please." I was ready for him to leave so I could focus on food for a sweet sixteen party. My mind wandered to cotton candy machine rentals and milkshake flavors.

He gave me an apologetic look. "I'm sorry if I've offended you. It's just that in all of my years of journaling, I've never met anyone... quite like you."

"Is that a compliment or an insult?" After spending time with Eloise Smarts, I'd learned to just ask outright.

He chuckled. "A compliment, of course! You Jenkins women are an extraordinary breed." His eyebrows waggled up and down. "Now what can you tell me about that Memaw. She's a real hoot, isn't she?"

When he left, I felt like I needed a nap. Instead, I energized with caffeine, chocolate, and Pinterest boards for sweet sixteen decorations.

•••••••

A week later, Hayes came into my office, holding the latest copy of *Little Peak Times* and a slice of Memaw's apple pie. He flashed me a smile, throwing the paper on the desk. "I'll let you enjoy this on your own."

"Oh, no, is it bad?" My stomach sank. But the pie looked good... I could still handle the pie.

"It's... sweet. I just know that you like to process things alone. That O'Malley is quite a character." He laid the plate and the paper on my desk. Giving me a kiss on the top of my head, he left my office.

Taking a deep breath, I lifted the paper. There, on the front page read the headline, *The Big Secret of CLAS Ranch.*

Pie forgotten, my stomach tied in knots. Had Mr. O'Malley found out about the Spanked Wives Club? Was he going to out our daddy dom lifestyle to the public? White heat slapped me in the face and I began to perspire.

*Everyone in Little Peak knows that at the top of town there sits a ranch. CLAS ranch. A place where people thrive on clean living and sunshine. A place that is home to a working cattle ranch as well as events.*

*The ranch has recently become famous for their five-star weddings. How does a cattle ranch in Podunk down in the middle of nowhere Wyoming find itself on the map of Top Ten destination weddings in the nation? It's a secret. And one that I'm going to share with you today.*

*Her name is Louanne Dixon.*

*Through hundreds of thousands of lists, Louanne has created the most elegant, memorable events to help people celebrate the important milestones in their lives. Has a family member of yours won a prestigious award? She has a trophy-themed brunch for that. Turning fifty? She'll throw you a black and white ball that will put your prom to shame. Overwhelmed by throwing your best friend's baby shower? She'll take over and make your friend want to have five more kids just to keep the parties coming.*

*Your little girl is getting married? Weddings just happen to be Louanne's specialty.*

*Louanne loves brides. To her, there is no such thing as a bridezilla, just a misunderstood woman trying to navigate the stressors of planning her big day.*

*The amount of time, attention, and love that Louanne invests in the milestones of people's lives is heartwarming. She finds joy in giving and in her mind if she hasn't created one of the best days of your life, then she hasn't done her job.*

He retold a few of the stories I had shared with him. I teared up at the quotes he had included from some of my favorite clients. The article went on to showcase the other employees of the ranch and how they assist with events.

I read the entire thing twice, smiling at the praise he hailed for our small team. Afterwards, I celebrated a job well done with the slice of pie.

• • • • • • •

As the weeks went by, I flew through my work practically gliding on air. There was such a thing as cloud nine, and I was on it. I had yet to make any real wedding plans for Hayes and me, but I was in no hurry. We were just reveling in our love, our lovemaking, and our engagement.

During the day, Hayes and I worked closely with one another, the attraction and flirting between us delicious. Then, when we couldn't take it anymore, we would sneak off for a rendezvous. We had discovered quite a few little hidden love nests on the ranch, indoors and out of doors. And of course, he had fixed the lock to my office.

Nights were spent doing much of the same, with a little eating and a few dates thrown in. We were both homebodies and were happy watching a movie on the couch together with takeout food.

And when we were home alone, that's when I could really revel in being a daddy's girl. Hayes would spoil me rotten, get me anything I wanted, rub my feet, dress me in soft pajamas. Call me baby girl, pretend I was being naughty, then flip me right over his lap for one of those sexy spankings that we both loved. They warmed my ass and had my pussy dripping by the time we finally made love.

The sexy spankings made me complacent. Made me forget about the other kinds of spankings daddies give their little girls. Soon enough, though, I would be reminded that if I didn't do as Hayes said, I would pay the price.

It all started when Hayes came into my office, greeting me with a kiss on my cheek. He took a seat in one of the chairs across from my desk. "Can we talk for a minute?"

"Sure. Let me just finish sending this email." I typed my closing regards and my name and hit 'send.' Closing my laptop, I said, "What's up?"

"It's about the article O'Malley wrote in the *Times*. It got me thinking," he said.

"That was weeks ago," I said.

"I've been mulling it over since then. Reading the article made me realize how much you carry on your plate, between the events and the weddings," he said.

"I love my job. I don't mind the hours," I said, brushing

away his concerns with a wave of my hand.

"I've been thinking about the way we are running things—and how many hours you work. It's no secret that you call pull a sixty-hour week some weeks and I think you need more help," he said.

"You mean, more part-time employees?" I asked.

"No. A full-time person. You need to hire someone to take over the legwork of the events. Someone you trust, that you can oversee, to do the day-to-day setting up, taking down, grunt work. You would still do all the planning and executing, you just wouldn't be the one completing the execution. It would allow you to work less hours and focus more on your passion—the weddings."

Someone else doing my job? No way. Things would fall apart if I wasn't the one carrying out my plans. "I don't think that's necessary, Hayes. I like doing everything myself."

"You would still have some creative control over all events. But like I said, you would have more time on your hands and be able to focus on what you love the most," he said.

"Does this have anything to do with the fact that we are now together, and you want us to spend more time with one another?" I asked.

"Selfishly, as your daddy, I want more time with you, yes. But, as your boss, I see the number of hours you work and I see the amount of money you generate. There is plenty to hire you an employee and take some things off your plate. As you would be supervising a full-time person, it would also mean a raise for you," he said.

I thought about it. It made perfect sense, one person to head up events, one to do the weddings. And before, I didn't mind working fifty or sixty hours a week—I had no social life whatsoever to speak of. But now that Hayes and I were dating, it would be nice to have some more free time to spend with him. But giving up control? I couldn't do it. "I see where you're coming from, but I don't think it's a good idea, Hayes. Let's keep things the way they are, now.

We can add another part-timer to the team, if you want to."

The tone of his voice hardened. "I'm not asking you. I'm telling you. This is the way I am restructuring the events department. I will oversee you, and you will oversee this person." His jaw clenched.

"Telling me as my boss, or my daddy?" I asked, crossing my arms over my chest.

His brow rose, his jaw tightening. "As your boss *and* your daddy, little girl."

I gave a nervous gulp as my panties dampened. "A little unprofessional, don't you think?" I squeaked.

"Not a bit. It's a family-run business. Lines get blurred," he stated.

"Is that so?" I asked.

"It is. Jenkins men look after their own. In business and in romance," he said.

"But I have your mom helping, and my sister, and at times, a dozen other part-time employees."

"We need someone full time underneath you to help manage those part-time employees," he said.

"What if I don't want a full-time employee?" I asked.

"Then I can hire them, oversee you both, and you can be co-chairs. But I'm guessing that is not what's best for you. Either way, we are hiring someone," he said.

Co-chairs over my cold, dead body. I was either the queen bee, or nothing. This business was my baby—I had seen it from the ground up, implementing and improving upon Brody's vision for the ranch with my own two hands. "Fine. But don't complain to me if I can't get along with someone else. I like things my way."

"I will be happy to administer an attitude adjustment in this very office at any moment you need one," he said.

I gulped. "So, if I don't carry out your plan and make it work... you are going to s-spank me? Is that even legal?"

He stood from his chair. Walking around the desk, he took my hand, pulling me up from my chair. Wrapping his arms around me, he leaned down, kissing me. He whispered into my ear, "We have our own set of laws here at CLAS ranch, and yes, it is very legal. Now, I believe you have a job to post." He kissed my forehead, patted my ass, and left my office.

I had other things to do. I still hadn't uploaded the photos from the last wedding to our website, and I had a ton of tidying to do before the magazine arrived. I decided the posting could wait.

# CHAPTER SIX

Hayes had to leave town for a few days. He was going to Jackson to meet with some of Alice's old friends. They owned Wyoming's Way, a line of all-natural skincare products that they made on their family ranch. Hayes was hoping to get them to agree to let CLAS distribute their lotions and cleansers in the Tack Shop, the soon to be built onsite gift shop.

It had been a long few days without my daddy. I had grown accustomed to seeing him several times though my day, and spending time with him every evening. I had missed him terribly while he was gone and could barely get to sleep without being tucked in.

He was due to arrive any moment, and I was in the Mess Hall, nibbling at a chicken tender, watching the door for him to enter.

Finally, the door swung open, and Hayes walked through. His eyes met mine, making my heart melt. I stood to greet him.

"Hi, Daddy," I said, reveling in the warmth of his hug. My cheek got all tingly when he gave it a soft kiss. "How'd the meeting go?"

"Great. We can now sell Judy's Wyoming's Way skincare

products in the Tack Shop," he smiled broadly. He buried his face in my hair, inhaling deeply. "I've missed that strawberry scent."

I laughed as he nibbled at my earlobe. "What Tack Shop? All that's there now is a pile of dirt."

"It will be there before you know it. I'm just waiting for the permits to come through from the town." He tucked a strand of my hair behind my ear, looking me over. "How'd the job post go?" he asked.

A queasy feeling entered my stomach. After Hayes had left my office the day he had requested the post, I had dove straight into uploading photos of my last wedding on the CLAS website. Then, I tackled planning the sweet sixteen party I had booked. It was my priority and completely took over any time I had to post the job. Every now and then, Hayes' request would cross my mind, but I didn't write the post.

There was also one tiny other detail I had not yet shared with Hayes—I had decided not to post the job. I knew I would need to eventually tell Hayes. For now, I sniffed indignantly, crossing my arms, and said, "I need more time to think about it."

He raised a brow to me. "More time to think about the wording of the post? I can help you with that."

The queasiness grew into a full-on sick feeling. "More time to think about whether there will be restructuring of my department," I said.

Clouds formed in his gaze. That little muscle in his jaw twitched. "Which is the department that I oversee and am ultimately responsible for. You were not given the option of thinking about it. You were given a very clear directive and asked to carry it out." Hayes' stern tone carried over the Mess Hall. I caught Bridgette and Georgia eyeing me with knowing looks on their faces.

My cheeks burned. Hayes could not boss me like this in front of other people. I had to stand my ground. I racked my mind for a quick comeback that would put him in his place. My temper flared, resulting in me snapping an uncharacteristic, "Whatever, Hayes." I turned on my heel, threw in a hair flip for good measure, and tromped across the Mess Hall floor.

As my hand reached toward the handle of the door, I was surprised by a firm grip around my upper arm, jolting my sassy exit to a stop.

Hayes' mouth was by my ear, his whispered words hard. "You cannot disrespect me like that in front of employees."

I froze, a shiver running down my spine. "But you just walked in the door from being gone two days and jumped right into bossing me around—"

"I was speaking to you in a respectful manner as a boss, correcting an employee who did not carry out the task they were given," he said.

What could I say in my defense? "I... I—"

"Meet me in your office in five minutes. And in case you are unclear—this is not a request. It is a command." I dared to peek up at his face. His strong jaw was clenched. There was not a hint of blue in his stormy gray eyes. Taking a gulp, I gave him a small nod.

Eyeing me, he said, "How about a 'yes, sir.'"

My stomach tied in knots. The independent woman in me fought with my suddenly submissive side. His grip tightened on my upper arm. A quiet "Yes, sir" escaped my lips.

He released me and I hurried off to my office, feeling dozens of curious eyes watching me as I went.

I had never felt more nervous than I did those few minutes waiting in my office for Hayes to come. I had no idea what to expect. I also had a very good idea of what to expect. My buttocks clenched in the seat beneath me.

He entered the office calmly, shutting and locking the door behind him. Standing before the door, he crossed his arms over his chest and gave me 'the look.'

My cheeks flushed. I began to stammer, "Look, I'm sorry, okay? I was angry and—"

"No excuses, Louanne," he said.

Anger flooded me. His stern tone and clenched jaw were a warning, but my temper ignored them. "Don't you dare tell me I'm making excuses. I said I was sorry and—"

"Lower your voice or I will lower your panties," he said.

My rant stopped, my words were left hanging in the air. My pussy clenched, my anger momentarily forgotten. My lips tried to form words of protest, but I was speechless. The good girl in me told me, "You've pushed him too far, Louanne. He's right. You spoke disrespectfully. Apologize and be done with it." But the bad girl... the bad girl wanted to test his limits. The bad girl wanted to push this angry cowboy. To see what he was made of. To know how far he would go. To piss him off. Bad girl Louanne whispered naughty things in my ear, daring me to say them. Finally, my mouth was working again. I stood up from my desk, saying, "Hayes, I am not having this conversation with you. You do not have the right to send me to my office like some child in a time out."

He remained silent. Though he was blocking the door, I decided that I would stride right out of my office. Or at least try to. I gave a gulp as I eyed his massive frame. Tilting my head in the air and feigning a bravery I did not feel, I began making my way toward the door. He did not move.

"Excuse me," I said indignantly, trying to push my way past him.

A long, muscular arm wrapped around my waist. My heart dropped into my stomach. His mouth was by my ear as he held me pressed against him. His words were calm, but angry. "Are you testing me, little girl?"

Trying to wriggle from his viselike grasp, I stuttered, "I... ah... no?"

"Now you're lying," he said.

"Okay, maybe I was testing you... a little bit," I admitted sheepishly.

"Ignoring my directives. Sassing me in front of employees. Testing me to see if I will carry out my words.

And lying when I called you on it. Was my two-day absence enough to make you forget who the boss is, here? Someone is overdue for a very long trip over my knee," he growled.

Reality was setting in. Judging by his tone, this was not going to be like the little sexy spanking he had given me in the Mess Hall before we got engaged. This was going to be a real punishment spanking. The ones that left Georgia sniffling and standing to eat her dinner. The ones that left Bridgette sullen for the rest of the day. Fear filled me. My stomach tied in knots. My knees were shaky. "I-I'm really sorry, Hayes. I'll go out and tell the employees I made a mistake."

"They'll know when you go back out, darling. You won't even have to tell them. After I spank you, you will be so sweet and docile they will know you've been properly punished," he said.

I froze. This was unacceptable. Having my employees know Hayes had spanked me in my office for sassing him? Sure, we had all been on the ranch a long time and knew how things worked, but it was different when I was the one on the receiving end of a Jenkins man's firm hand at work. How humiliating. Grabbing Hayes' shoulders, I looked into his very gray stern eyes and begged, "Please don't spank me! I promise I'll never be sassy again. I would die if I had to go back out there afterwards, everyone knowing—"

"Too late. You should have thought of that before. At least you can take solace in one little fact," he said.

"Wha-what's that?" I stammered.

His gaze studied my face. "Knowing you have a daddy to discipline you when you're bad."

He was going to spank me—for real—right here in my office. What if people could hear him spanking me? What if I cried and had to go back out there sniffling like Georgia? What if I couldn't sit down the rest of the day? I had lists to write, plans to make! My hands dropped from his shoulders.

Slowly, I inched backwards trying to get away from him. The move was useless and stupid, but it was instinctual. I tried to make a distance between us. He stayed where he was, standing like a big, looming statue of solid rock. "Where are you going?" he asked. I detected a hint of amusement in his tone.

I took one more step, my bottom bumping into the desk behind me. "Oompf!" I stopped, my hands clutching the edges of the desk that my ass was pressed against. "Nowhere," I replied sweetly.

Approaching me, his stride reminded me of a panther prowling toward his prey. My breath quickened, my heart raced. My wide eyes stared up into Hayes' incredibly handsome, incredibly pissed-off face. I gulped, leaning back, pressing my hands into the desk.

With his face inches from mine and his voice low, he said, "You were naughty in the Mess Hall. It was a childish display. And what am I to do with a bad little girl?"

"Um... maybe just let her get back to work?" I squeaked.

"You were naughty. And now everyone knows you are in here having the sass spanked right out of you by your daddy. How does that feel?" he asked.

"Humiliating." And yet, my nipples were hardening, the muscles within my pussy were tightening. I was horny as hell. And nervous.

"Let that be a lesson to you next time you want to sass me. Now how shall I punish you? Over the desk? Over my knee? Or take you out to the Mess Hall and spank you in front of your employees?" he asked.

Horror ran though me. White heat spread across my face. My ass dug harder into the edge of the desk. I pictured myself over Hayes' knee, the entire ranch looking on as he spanked me. "No, no... no... anything but that!"

Was he trying to hide a grin? "Then how do you want it, Luna? Over my knee? Bent over your desk like the naughty girl that you are? Using my hand? The first time you sassed me, I used the wooden spoon. Obviously, it didn't make a good enough impression. Maybe I should use that wooden ruler you so love. The one you keep in your desk drawer?"

I gasped. How dare he! That was my sacred wedding prep tool! My cheeks were absolutely on fire at this point. I quickly stammered, "Over your knee with your hand, please!"

"I bet you'd never thought you'd be begging for a spanking, did you?" he said.

"I... I'm not—I just... you said that about my ruler and the Mess Hall and I—"

"Shh. Let's get you over my knee, little thing. I can already see the sass leaving you," he said.

Balls of ice formed in my stomach. I couldn't do this. I couldn't be spanked in my office. Peeking over his shoulder at the door, I quickly formulated a plan. "Okay. I'll just go over to that chair right there and wait for you." Avoiding his eyes, I slid sideways along the desk, creeping around him. As soon as I had cleared him, I made a break for the door.

"Oompf!" Again, the long strong arm reached out, stopping me.

"Naughty girl. Trying to run away from your punishment? Now it's going to be my hand *and* the ruler."

"I was just... no, Hayes, please. Not my ruler. I use it for weddings to make sure each candle is exactly the same distance apart. It would feel so unprofessional," I wailed.

"I will spank you with your ruler. And you will continue to use it. And it will remind you of what happens when you try to boss the boss. Now go and get it. Please." He released his hold on me.

Nerves danced up and down my spine. I squeaked out, "I have to get it... myself?"

"Yes. Now."

Not wanting to make more trouble for myself, I hurried over to the desk drawer. Heaving a deep sigh, I pulled it open. There lay my precious old-fashioned wooden ruler with its trusty metal edge. Great for penciling lines on paper and measuring distances. And now, doubling as a tool for my punishment. My fingertips felt icy as I reached down in the drawer, lifting out my ruler.

My knees slightly shaking, I returned to Hayes. He had pushed one of two club chairs I kept across from my seat at the desk for my clients out and back. His long lean frame sat in the chair, his legs spread as if he were the king of the place.

This would never do! Those were my client chairs! This was my candle ruler!

I stopped a few feet short of Hayes. "I, I can't do this, Hayes."

"You can, Luna. And you will." He patted his left knee. "Now come on over here and put that pretty little ass over my knee."

My face lit on fire. I buried it in my hands, the ruler still clutched between my fingers. I wailed, "I can't!"

His impatient voice boomed through my office. "Do I need to count, young lady?"

My hands dropped from my face, my eyes widening. "Wha-what happens if you count?"

His brow rose. His lips tightened, forming an angry line. "When I count, you come. If I get to three," his gaze bore into mine as his fingertip tapped at his silver belt buckle, "my belt comes off."

I lost my breath. Forgetting my apprehension, I scurried over to where he sat. I stood by his side, my knees brushed against his thigh. I had no idea what to do. Usually, Hayes had all control of the situation and put me over his knee himself. Having to put myself into position? It was too much. I stood there, shifting my weight from foot to foot, trying to decide the most ladylike way to go about it.

"Oompf!"

Hayes, apparently impatient with my indecision, took it upon himself to flip me over his lap. His hands grasped my waist tightly, pulling me right over his knee. Scrambling, I pressed my hands into the floor, trying to maintain my balance and not flip right off him, though with the viselike grip he had around my waist, I doubted it was possible.

My hair fell around my face, the blood rushing to my

head as I hung upside down. Hayes was much taller than me and once I was spread over his lap, my tippy toes could not reach the floor. My legs hung, suspended from his thigh. My tummy hurt from nerves, my heart beat hard against my ribcage.

"Comfy?" Hayes asked with a chuckle. I must have looked a sight to him, hanging over his legs, my bottom perched over his thigh.

"Hayes, I… I do not think this is appropriate! My office? You already know how I feel about the ruler—"

"Ahh, yes, my ruler. Where did it go?" he asked.

It had fallen when I released it to put my hands on the floor and steady myself. From where I hung, I could see it peeking out from under the legs of my furniture style file cabinet. "I think I lost it when you flipped me over," I said.

"There will be time for you to find it. After I warm you up with my hand." His hand lightly patted my bottom three little times. Goosebumps rose on my legs. The muscles in my pussy tightened. God, I loved it when he touched my ass—though I wasn't sure I was going to like it as much when he was spanking it with my ruler. "Let's start over your skirt, shall we?"

"Erm?" Was this to be a bare bottom spanking? Panic rose in my chest… what panties was I wearing?

"The first spanking—the one with my hand—is for sassing me in the Mess Hall. After your bottom is properly punished, I want you sitting in your desk chair, sniffling and writing up the post for the full-time position. Is that clear?"

"Yes, sir!" I called up from the floor.

"Good girl. I'm going to start with a warmup spanking since you are still slightly new to this whole 'being held accountable for unruly behavior with a paddling' thing."

"You would assume correctly—because I am always such a well-behaved person!" I cried.

He laughed, "Not today, you weren't. You were a very bad little girl. Are you ready for your spanking?"

Is one ever ready for a spanking? Better to keep that

comment to myself. I managed to stammer, "Y-yes?"

"Yes, sir?" he asked.

Ugh. I wanted to roll my eyes but felt like Hayes would somehow sense the action and punish me more. Instead, I said, "Yes, sir."

"Little Luna, getting her first office spanking. Maybe I should take a picture to remember this moment." He moved as if he was reaching into the pocket of his jeans for his phone.

My head snapped back, trying to see him over my shoulder. "Hayes—no! You have to be kidding!"

Three little pats on my bottom had my pussy tightening and my nipples peaked beneath my bra. "Maybe next time. Now for the spanking."

I squeezed my eyes shut tight and held my breath. My bottom cheeks clenched together as I anticipated a hard spank. I could feel his hand go up in the air, hovering over my bottom. His hand came down on my right ass cheek, over my skirt-covered bottom. The sound echoed through the room. My bottom tingled where his hand had landed. It wasn't painful, but instead had my pussy aching and my nipples hardened. His hand rose again and landed on the left cheek. The same tingling covered my skin. My pussy gave another squeeze.

If this was what a punishment felt like, sign me up for misbehaving. Another spank came down, my panties dampening. My hips wiggled a bit. I was so turned on. Then a harder spank landed. This one made me suck in my breath a little. Before I could recover, another one landed, harder, right in the same place as the first! I protested, "Hayes! That hurt."

He laughed at me. "Luna—I haven't even warmed you up yet."

My eyes widened as another two hard spanks were applied to my bottom. My hips shifted as I groaned, the stinging covering my bottom. Then Hayes started spanking me. His hand went up and down, over and over again. The spanks were hard and fast. Tears pricked at my eyes. I could only focus on the burning pain that was my bottom. No more sexy feeling—this was now clearly a punishment. Hayes began to lecture me as I tried not to cry out from the spanks.

"I told you to post the job. Days later I find out you did no such thing—and you tell me you won't. Have you changed your mind about that, yet?" he asked.

If my mind hadn't changed, the hard, fiery spanks that were landing faster and faster on my bottom were sure changing it fast. "Yes—I'll post it right away, sir!" I wasn't sure how much more I could take, but the spanks kept coming down in a loud, rhythmic cadence.

"And I don't like when my little girl has a sassy mouth. All good daddies know how to correct a sassy mouth. And that is with a good old-fashioned spanking. Are you still feeling sassy, sweetheart?"

"No! No, sir! I'm really not," I assured him from between clenched teeth. Two more spanks landed, then he stopped. I hung over his lap, panting and trying to catch my breath. I cried, "Oh, thank goodness that is over!"

"Did you forget about the ruler?" he asked.

I had! "Oh, Hayes, I've learned my lesson, I promise! We do not need the ruler!"

Hayes helped me up from his lap. He stood me next to him, his eyes watching me as my hands went to my bottom, attempting to rub out the sting. "I still have to spank you for trying to run away from me."

I looked at him earnestly, saying, "No, no. I've learned my lesson. I promise!"

He considered my face for a moment, before he spoke. "I'll tell you what. Since it's your first time with the ruler, I'll let you keep your panties on. I am a gentleman after all."

I opened my mouth to protest. His brow rose in the most threatening way and after second thought, I snapped my lips closed. Leaving his side, I scurried over to the file cabinet, bending over and retrieving the ruler. I brought it back to him.

"Good girl," he crooned. "Now let's get you back over my knee." As before, he grabbed my hips, flipping me over his lap. My hands went back to the floor, my hair spilling over my face. I bit my lower lip, squeezing my eyes shut tight in shame as I felt his hand go to the hem of my A-lined skirt. He flipped it up and over my bottom. Cold air rushed up my bare legs. The sensation of having my bottom exposed, wearing only panties, overwhelmed me. A sudden sense of... belonging... filled my chest. Lying over Hayes' lap, in his complete control, my ass exposed, I felt as if he owned me, mind, body, and soul. Knowing what was coming, I still let a small smile cross my lips. Georgia was right—being spanked was sexy as hell.

I waited for the ruler to bite my skin. There was a whoosh, then down it came, onto the curve of my bottom, the part that was the least covered by my panties. It stung much worse than his hand had. A line of fire slowly crept across my ass where the ruler had struck. I gave a whimpering, "Yeowie!" All thoughts of sexy were gone! The pain was blinding!

My bottom was still stinging from his hand spanking, 'warmed up' as he had said. The ruler came down again with a sharp snap, this time striking the center of my right cheek. My hips shifted, my feet pressing together as I absorbed the stinging spank. I gave another whimper as the ruler came down on the left cheek. It stung much worse than I had anticipated. Tears sprang in my eyes—I would soon be sniffling as Hayes had promised.

"Are you going to be my very good little girl from now on?" he asked, the ruler making another smack.

"Yes, sir!" I cried from between clenched teeth. "I've learned my lesson—no sassing and no running away!"

The ruler came down again. I sucked air in between my teeth, my feet rubbing together.

"And next time you are naughty and need a spanking, are you going to put yourself over my knee?" he asked, bringing the ruler down again.

My hips wiggled furiously, my hands wanting to reach back and rub at my poor, stinging ass. I cried out, "Yes, Daddy! I will put myself right over your knee anytime you want if you never use this ruler on me again!"

The punishment stopped. I breathed a sigh of relief, closing my eyes and relaxing. The moment quickly passed as I felt my panties sliding over my sore bottom.

"Daddy, you said you would leave the panties on for the ruler!" I cried.

"I did," he said.

"So... what are you doing, now?" I wailed.

"This daddy knows his little girl very, very well. And even though you are apologizing, I can still detect just a hint of defiance in your voice. I intend to draw out your full submission." With that, his hand came down in a sharp spank. Tears brimmed in my eyes as I wailed. He spanked me again and again. The tears fell from my eyes. I could focus on nothing but the pain. I hung limply and sobbed as he spanked my sore bottom. When I thought it would never end, he finally pulled my panties back into place over my throbbing bottom.

His hand patted my panties. I heaved a giant sigh of relief as his hands went to the fabric of my skirt, pulling it up and over me. "There. I'm done, sweetheart. Come here."

He helped me up and onto his lap. I wound my arms around his neck, burying my face in the collar of his shirt. He smelled like clean laundry and man. I let my tears flow freely into the fabric of his shirt. I hadn't expected the release of tension that followed the spanking. My ass burned—I wiggled it on his thighs every so often trying to escape the inescapable sting—but I loved the new-to-me sensation that washed over me. I felt small, protected, chastised, loved. And as he'd intended, submissive.

My pussy started that clenching thing again as his fingertips trailed up and down my back as I recovered from my punishment. He kissed my hair, my forehead, my cheek.

His hands wiped at my tear-streaked face. I looked up into his blue-gray eyes. Overcome by emotion, I whispered, "I love you, Hayes."

"I love you too, sweetheart." He kissed the tip of my nose. "I hate to leave you, but I've got to get back to work and check in with the guys and tell them about the Tack Shop." His brow rose at me. "And you have a job to post."

I sniffled.

Chuckling, he stood me on my feet. A sadness rushed over me—I wanted to sit snuggled on his lap the rest of the day. And I had missed him so much while he'd been gone. I didn't want him to leave my office. Standing beside me, Hayes grabbed the ruler in one of his hands and my hand in the other. He led me back to my desk. Pulling out my drawer, he reverently placed my ruler back in its exact spot. Gently, he closed the drawer. Then, he pulled out my desk chair.

His hand still holding mine, he looked at me and said, "Skirt up."

My brow furrowed, I asked, "What do you mean?"

"Gather your skirt around your waist and take a seat in your chair. When you are writing the job posting, I want your mind to be on what happens when you disobey my instructions," he said.

A warm blush crept up my neck as I followed his instructions. As Hayes had predicted, all sassiness had been spanked out of me. I did as he said, folding my skirt up best I could to keep it from wrinkling. The cold air once again rushed up my legs. I sat down in the hard wooden chair a little too quickly. I winced as my punished bottom hit the seat.

Hayes gave me a kiss on the top of my head. "I love you, sweetie. Enjoy your work."

Sighing, I flipped open the top to my computer. Where to begin? *Help wanted... someone who will do exactly as told per the instruction of the events coordinator, otherwise creating friction that might result in getting said coordinator spanked with a measuring ruler.*

Despite my sore bottom, I had to smile. The burning had turned to more of a tingling warmth, making me horny all over again. The dominance he had shown over me, taking me to my breaking point, demanding my submission—it had me wanting him more than ever.

Flipping me over his knee like that… taking me in hand… it was so. Damn. Sexy. My hips wiggled in my chair, my pussy clenching and pulsing in a melty way. Shaking my head, I tried to ignore my desire and focus on the post—as good as my pussy felt, my ass pressed against the hard chair was not ready to revisit the ruler just yet.

I typed away. Every so often my mind wandered to the fact that I was sitting on my panty-covered bottom, freshly spanked by my daddy, and my pussy would tighten.

Once I was happy with my work, I checked my complexion in the small mirror I kept in my desk. My eyes were a little puffy from my cry. The tip of my nose a touch red. Reaching into my drawer, I got out my pressed powder. A few dabs later and I looked good as new. Surely, no one would be able to tell that I had been spanked. Right? Shrugging my shoulders, I shoved down the embarrassing thought.

Coffee and triple chocolate cake were waiting for me in the Mess Hall—promised by Memaw since it was one of the ranch hand's birthdays. Checking the time, I stood from my desk, my face burning as I put my skirt back in place—thank goodness no one had walked in as I typed the ad. I couldn't imagine someone finding the uptight, prissy Louanne Dixon sitting at her desk, skirt up and around her waist.

The thought made me… thirsty. And only Hayes could quench the thirst. I sat back down.

Tapping my fire engine red fingernail on the desk, I contemplated. It was completely unprofessional to call your daddy over the walkie for a booty call. I squirmed in my chair, my pussy pulsing and wet. But it was professional to handle something that was keeping you from focusing on your work. I just needed a good, hard banging, then I could get right back to the old grindstone. I picked up my walkie. "Hayes... Louanne for Hayes."

His voice came cracking over the radio. "Copy, Hayes."

"Could I see you in my office for a minute? I need some help with the wording of this post." I giggled to myself getting a kick out of thinking about what Bridgette and Georgia would have to say about that one later. The nosy girls were probably already beside themselves wondering what had happened when Hayes drug me out of the Mess Hall earlier.

I could hear a grin in Hayes' voice when he came back over the walkie. "Copy, Luna. Be right there."

I hopped up from my chair, rushing to the front of my desk. I leaned back on it, trying to position my body in what I felt like was a seductive stance. I glanced down at my buttoned-up blouse. Quickly, I undid the top two buttons, opening the shirt a bit until my cleavage peeked out of the top.

A few minutes later the door opened. Hayes appeared. Was that a bulge already forming underneath his pants? My question was answered when he crossed the room and pressed himself against me for a kiss. My hand ran over his hardening cock, my pussy screaming for it.

His hand wrapped around the back of my neck, pulling me in for a hard kiss. His lips pressed against mine. I matched his hunger, eagerly returning his kiss. His hand found my breast, sliding beneath the top of my shirt and under my bra. I sucked in air as his fingertips pinched my peaked, hardening nipple. "Naughty girl," he growled.

His hand slipped under my skirt, fingertips brushing against my pussy over my damp panties. "Let's see how wet your pussy got from your spanking, little Luna. Did Daddy make you wet when he took you over his knee and spanked your bare bottom?"

I shuddered, moving my hips forward, trying to gain some purchase of his hand against my clit. He continued to tease me, rubbing my pussy lightly with just the tip of his finger. I groaned.

"Naughty, naughty little thing. Patience. Daddy wants to see how wet you are from your spanking, first." His fingers slipped beneath the elastic of the leg of my panties. "Someone's panties got wet. Do you need to change your panties, little girl?"

I moaned.

"Daddy asked you a question. Do you need to go home and put on fresh panties?"

"No, Daddy," I moaned.

His finger moved up the slippery folds of my pussy. My eyes rolled in the back of my head as he rubbed my throbbing, pulsing clit. I leaned my head back, moaning.

"Just as I suspected. Daddy spanking you makes your pussy get very, very wet." My hips gyrated, my clit rubbing hard against his finger as he moved it against me. His finger left my clit, sliding down. I groaned again as he moved it in and out. My pussy tightened around him. "So wet. Such a dirty girl getting off on her punishment." A second finger joined his first, stretching me. His fingers moved within me. My pelvis rocked as I rode his hand. "Maybe spanking isn't enough of a punishment for you, little one."

My hips froze, my eyelids fluttering open in surprise. What other ways could he—would he—punish me? Butterfly wings trembled in my tummy. "What do you mean?"

One of his fingers slipped out of my pussy. The other remained, fingering me up and down. The missing member stretched upward. I gasped in shock and horror as his fingertip pressed on my anus. "Sometimes when naughty little girls get too excited by their spankings, their daddies have to find other ways to punish them."

My eyes squeezed shut tight. My cheeks burned with shame. My pussy tightened around his finger with another gush of excitement. His finger slipped into my ass up to what felt like the first knuckle. I held my breath as his hot words whispered in my ears. "Sometimes, daddies have to punish by putting a big hard cock in your tight little bottom, teaching you the ultimate submission."

Never had I ever participated in anal play. That was something good girls did not do. Absolutely not. Yes, I had done lots of dirty deeds with Hayes—I called him 'Daddy,' for goodness' sake!—and yes, they had all given me extreme pleasure. And yes, I lay over my man's knee, begging him to spank me. But up the butt? That was crossing a line of taboo I wasn't ready for.

Or was I? His finger slipped out of my ass and I instantly wanted it back in. I wanted him to pump it further inside me, I wanted to see what it felt like to be taken there. My pussy told on me, tightening and pulsing and weeping. I had to have him... now. "I need you to fuck me," I begged.

His free hand reached up, grabbing my chin in his hands. "Dirty mouth for such a little girl. Does Daddy need to spank you again?"

"No, sir. Let me show you what I can do with this dirty little mouth of mine," I said.

His eyes lit with desire. His fingers slid from within me. My hands went to the waist of his jeans, unbuttoning them. I reached down, taking his cock in my hand. It was big and hard, and I wanted it inside of me. Flashing me a wicked smile, he pushed his jeans down over his ass. I bent down, taking his cock in my mouth. I licked my tongue around the tip, swirling and twirling as he groaned with satisfaction. His hands found their way into my hair. He gathered the hair on the back of my neck and tugged while I sucked him. I grabbed his balls in my hands, fondling them as I mouthed up and down his shaft.

"Damn, Luna. That feels amazing." He pulled me back up toward him, grabbing my face in his hands and kissing me deeply. He moved our bodies backwards until I bumped into the edge of my desk. His hands were all over me, squeezing my breasts, squeezing my ass underneath my skirt. He pulled my panties down to my knees. I quickly shimmied out of them, kicking them off and onto the floor—I had learned to keep a spare in my desk drawer.

Hayes' hands wrapped underneath my bottom, grabbing and squeezing my ass cheeks. I giggled as he lifted me up and onto the desk. He kissed my cheek, nibbled my ear. His mouth trailed down my neck, biting and sucking until a groan escaped my lips. I arched my back, my pelvis forward, ready for his cock.

The head of his cock was suddenly pressing into my opening. I lifted my hips, moaning and moving closer to him, begging him to put it in me. I wanted all of him, mind, body, soul. I wanted our bodies connected as one. And I wanted his full cock buried deep within me.

"Patience, baby girl," he whispered, nipping at my earlobe. He continued to tease me, slowly pressing into me inch by inch.

"More," I begged, throwing my neck back. He kissed and licked and sucked and bit the hollow I had created for him above my collarbone. I shuddered with desire and delight, tingles dancing down my spine. Finally, with one carnal thrust, his full member was within me. I groaned, grinding down on his rod. My hips twisted and rocked, the edge of my bottom barely leaning on the desk as my pussy demanded everything his cock could give me.

His arms wrapped around my lower back tightly, as he lifted me into the air. My legs wrapped around his torso as if I would squeeze the life from him, I needed him so badly. He thrust his hips up, pressing his huge cock into me. We moved together as one, me crying, "Harder, faster." The impending explosion began to grow within my core. My nipples were as tight as drums, my pussy clenching and pulsing and milking his cock in ecstasy. I could no longer think. My breath caught in my chest. My eyelids locked shut and I bit my bottom lip until it bled as I held in the scream that came with his final thrust. I shuddered as he held me against him, my hair damp and stuck to my face. "Oh, Daddy," I whisper, my lips finding his once more.

When he left, I pulled a spare panty from the drawer and

snuck off to the bathroom to clean up.

Leaving the restroom, grinning ear to ear, I began my walk to the Mess Hall. The weather was gorgeous, and the spring air felt fresh against my face. My bottom was still sore and my pussy still tingling as I crunched my way over the rocky drive. As I neared the Mess Hall, I began to get nervous. Everyone had seen me sass Hayes. And seen him lead me away by my upper arm. And heard me call for him on the walkie. I felt like they could see my reddened bottom through my skirt. Smell the sex on me.

Standing at the door, I hesitated, my hand hovering over the handle of the door. Everyone would look at me, knowing I had been spanked and taken by Hayes. But there was triple chocolate cake in there. And hot coffee with fresh cream. As I stood, making my decision, a big arm suddenly surrounded my waist. I looked up, laughing as Hayes pulled me into a surprise embrace. His kissed my mouth, then whispered in my ear, "Did you get your work done?"

"Yes," I murmured, melting into his embrace.

His hand went to my bottom, squeezing my sore cheek and sending me up on my tiptoes. "And how's your ass?"

"Good," I giggled, blushing.

"Then let's get you some cake," he said with a grin. He released me, holding the door opened for me. He said, "After you."

I took a deep breath, casting my eyes downward as we entered the crowded Mess Hall. Everyone had come out to wish Bo a happy birthday. I stood tight against Hayes' side, hiding under the protection of his big arm. Georgia gave me a wink and a wave. Bridgette gave me an eyebrow wiggle, mouthing the words, "How's your ass?" which I ignored. But other than that, it was business as usual at the ranch. Another day, another spanked woman.

# CHAPTER SEVEN

"This weekend went great, don't you think?" Josie asked, taking a huge bite of her greasy, cheesy burger. The girl ate whatever she wanted when she wanted, existing off of coffee the rest of the time, and never gained an ounce.

The prongs of my fork sorted through the greens of my salad—no cheese, dressing on the side—after Memaw's cake, I was feeling guilty. "So, what was this 'SOS you have to meet me for dinner tonight' text that I got from you all about?"

Josie shrugged her shoulders, dragging a fry through a puddle of ketchup. "Just checking in, seeing what's going on."

Raising my brows at her, I said, "That is not a reason for an SOS, Josie." I stole one of her fries, waiting for the real reason we were meeting.

"What? Can't a little sister meet her big sister for a little sisterly advice, sister?" she asked, giving me her 'spoil me, please,' smile. I could still picture her as a skinned-kneed little girl in pigtails, tagging along behind me and my friends.

"Cut the sister crap. Just tell me… what do you want?" I asked, laughing at her expressive face and helping myself to another fry.

Josie gave a sigh, rolling her eyes. She pushed her plate toward me. "Ugh, I'm stuffed. And that salad looks... droopy. You want the rest?"

I eyed her food. There were at least seven hundred calories left on her plate—and they looked delicious. On one hand I was recently engaged. I should probably try to keep my figure looking trim so I would be able to fit into a dress. On the other hand, I was engaged to a spanking daddy. Which meant I could use a little extra padding on the old behind. I reached over, grabbing the burger. I took a bite. It was delicious. And so much better than my slightly wilted salad.

Between bites, I said, "Okay. You've got me buttered up. Now, lay it on me. What is so important that we had to meet tonight?"

She gave me her sweetest smile. "I just need a little advice."

"About what?" I asked, washing the burger down with a sip of her Coke.

"It's job advice," she answered quietly. Was she blushing?

"Okay—did you finally find one? I know Mom's been after you. She told me she gave you an ultimatum—find full-time work or apply to colleges. Did you make a decision?" I asked, taking another fry.

"I found this awesome full-time job. It pays well, has benefits—which you know are impossible to find these days—and the boss is like, the absolute best at what she does. I could learn, like so, so much from her." Josie's eyebrows waggled up and down at me.

I put the burger down, a knot forming in my stomach. "How did you see it already? I just put it up this afternoon!"

Her eyes widened, a light sparking within them. "I check the ranch's website every day. Twice a day actually. I knew once Hayes came back to CLAS there was no way he would let you keep working the hours you were—"

"Wait... what do you mean, 'let me'? Hayes and I made

this decision together," I said.

She gave me a long, hard look. "Really?"

I gave her 'the look.'

Which she ignored. Taking a deep breath, she said, "The whole ranch knows Hayes spanked your ass in the office today. And about an hour later the job was posted. So, if I put the pieces together started with when you sassed him in the Mess Hall this morning, I would guess that Hayes told you this was happening, you told him 'no' in your little control freak way, then he changed your mind via smacking your ass—"

I held up my hand to her. "Enough, Josie."

She stopped. It looked like she was in physical pain from trying to hold her tongue. "Anyway, as I was saying, I had been checking the website, *anticipating* that soon a job would be up to help out with events. And, today was that day!" She bounced up and down in her seat, clapping her hands.

I gave a sigh. "I love you, Josie. But it wouldn't be professional. I can't have my family working for me."

"Really?" She gave me a dirty look.

"Stop saying 'really' to me. And the next time you try to get someone to hire you, you might want to be a tad less rude," I said.

"I gave you my burger, just hear me out, K? Georgia is married to Brody—she works for Travis. Bridgette is married to Travis and helps Colton. Alice is the mother to all the boys, and she used to work for you. And Memaw is the matriarch and she's the boss of all the Jenkinses. So, why wouldn't it work out for me to work for you? I do good work, don't I?" she asked in a small voice. Her pretty brown eyes were huge and glassy as she looked at me with a puppy-like gaze.

I loved Josie. And she did a pretty good job on the ranch. But, I had major reservations about her going full time, especially with me as her direct boss. Choosing my words carefully, I began my respectful decline. "Honey, I think it's time you find what you are passionate about. Take some courses at college, get an idea of what you want to do with your life."

"I'm passionate about the ranch! It's like my... home away from home. I practically grew up there and I love helping out with stuff. And, you know how much I struggled through school. I would flunk out of college and waste all of Mom's money," she sighed.

It was true—I had spent many tearful afternoons at the kitchen table trying to help her through her homework. Josie was incredibly street smart and life skills savvy but she had trouble with learning from books. But working for me? Full time? "Josie, I worry about being your boss. I think I'm too lenient on you at times. It could cause... friction."

"I would do a great job. I promise. Please hire me," she begged.

"I need someone really organized," I said.

"I'm not like you, Louie. I don't have a plan for my life and seventeen lists each step of the way. But I know I want this job. And that I'd be great at it," she said.

I hated to disappoint her, but I had to be honest. "You come in late sometimes. You leave a little early. You don't dress professionally enough. And those tattoos, sometimes I don't think they are very appropriate for weddings."

Her eyes became cold. "You don't like my tattoos?"

"I didn't say that. But see, even this." I waved my hands between us. "I can't offer you constructive criticism without you getting angry."

Her face softened. "I see your point." She bit her bottom lip, her brow furrowing. After a moment of studying her straw wrapper, she said, "What about this, Louie—you take me on a trial basis. I'll get some more appropriate clothing—even long-sleeved if you want. I'll be early, I'll stay late. Give me one month and then make your decision. Could you do that? Just take that job posting down, tonight. Let me try the job out at my part-time rate, you can pay me by the hour, and in one month, if I do a bad job, I'll find something else and you can post the job. What do you say?

Huh? Pretty please?"

I considered her face. She was eager, a hard worker—once she actually made it to the ranch—and the guests absolutely loved her. My resolve began to melt. "I have to talk to Hayes."

Her brows rose in surprise. "Okay—that's okay. Talk to Hayes—put in a good word for me—then let me know ASAP, K?"

I laughed. "Okay. I will. But don't get your hopes up too high." I had a feeling Hayes was not going to love this plan as much as Josie did.

"I won't. I promise," she said.

Though I was not eager to bring this idea up to Hayes, I was ready to crawl in bed with him. I would take the posting down and talk to him about Josie tomorrow at work. Tonight was for other, much more pleasurable things. I grabbed the check off the table. "I guess I'm paying, huh? Seeing as you don't have a full-time job, yet?"

"But maybe soon," she smiled, hopping up from the booth.

We would see.

• • • • • • •

A few days later, a very angry cowboy barged into my office. Hayes stood before my desk, eyes deep gray, jaw clenched tightly. His hands went to the buckle of his belt.

Oh, dear. I had completely forgotten to tell him about Josie's trial run. I gulped as he growled, "The job posting has been taken down. There had better be a very good reason for this, Louanne, or so help me, I am taking off this belt and you will be standing at your desk the rest of the—"

I hopped up from my chair, rushing over to him. Stammering, I interrupted his threat—though I was very curious to see what that leather would feel like against my bare skin. "There is a good reason. I promise." I forced my way into his arms. He stood rigid, putting his arms stiffly around me.

"There had better be, little girl, start talking."

I kissed his cheek, his neck. I could feel the muscles of his body softening as I stroked his shoulders. "It is a good reason. I promise. I think I already found a candidate, so I took the job posting down."

He pulled away, looking down at me with a furrowed brow. "Who?"

"She's a cute little blonde. Vivacious, has great spirit. Works very hard when she wants to—"

His gaze clouded over. "Does she happen to have a tattoo of a butterfly on her upper arm and one in the shape of the state of Florida on her forearm?" he asked.

The look he gave me made me want to lie. I opted for a, "*Maybe*?"

Hayes took my arms down from around his neck, placing them at my sides. "No way, Luna. Not Josie? You have to be kidding me."

"What? She's my sister! And she is a good worker—"

"When she actually shows up on time. No way, this is not happening," he said.

"But Hayes, hear me out. She knows she's a risk and that it might not work—especially with me as her sister being her boss—so she made a plan," I said.

His brows rose in vague disinterest. "Josie Dixon has a plan?"

"Yes. And it's not half bad. Just listen." After heaving a sigh, he gave me a nod. I continued, "I take the posting down. She works the job for one month—at her part-time hourly rate. At the end of the month, if *we* decide she isn't the right candidate, she quits. What do you think?" I wrapped my arms back around his neck, smiling adoringly up at him.

He considered my face for a long minute. "I'm against the plan. I think Josie can be a bit immature at times and you are much too lenient on her. This is a very busy time for us. I don't think we can risk giving her a chance and losing a client if she doesn't work out. But also, I trust your judgement."

"I understand—and share—all of your concerns. But she is my sister. She grew up on this ranch. She's my family, and yours too. Please, Hayes?" I asked softly.

Hope fluttered in my heart as a hint of a smile appeared on his face. "Tell you what. We try her out for one month. She makes any mistakes, and it's your ass on the line." He gave my ass a sharp slap. "Literally."

So, I would be getting spanked if Josie messed up. Great. That second doughnut I had turned down at breakfast now seemed like a mistake—I was going to need the extra padding. At least I finally got to tell my little sister she was in. Now, maybe her one thousand 'did Hayes say yes yet' text messages would slow down.

●  ●  ●  ●  ●  ●  ●

"Really? I got it?" Josie cried, clapping her hands. Her white-blonde hair was piled high on top of her head, the sleeve of her black tank top hanging down over her shoulder. She was not wearing a bra. Her favorite sweatpants hung down low around her hips, exposing her taut belly. She looked like what we Dixon women call a 'hot mess.'

What had I done?

Feigning confidence, I managed a tightlipped smile and a, "Yes."

Her pretty brown eyes lit up. "Really, really?"

Her excitement was contagious. Pushing away thoughts of my huge cowboy boss threatening to spank me if she messed up, I laughed. "Yes, really, really!"

Leaping over the piles of clothes on her floor, she wrapped her arms around me, digging into my ribcage. She was strong for being so little! Her eyes shone as she released me, stammering, "Thank you, Louie! Thank you so much!

I'm not going to let you down. I promise. You are going to be so proud of me. Just wait and see. At the end of this month you are going to hire me. I just know it. Tell Hayes thank you, too! I have to go text Colton. He's going to be so excited." She started to leave the room to get her phone.

"Whoa—slow down, Josie. Why would you need to tell Colton? Couldn't you just tell him tomorrow, at the ranch?" I asked.

Her creamy complexion turned a pretty pink as she blushed. "Well, I just think he'll want to know sooner."

"Why?" I demanded.

Her hands went to her hair, nervously patting at the rat's nest that sat there. "Because we are… talking."

My stomach turned. "What does *talking* mean?" I asked.

"You know… it's just a little friend-y thing… like, texting each other. I had to get his number the other day for a friend that wanted lessons and you know it just kind of started this cute little flirtatious back and forth thing. I mean, we talk at work, but we've never texted one another. It's so fun. I told him my plan about the job and he said he hoped I'd get it and that he would love for me to be on the ranch more," she said.

"How serious is this 'little friend-y thing' with Colton?" I was already worried about overseeing my sister. I didn't want to also be wrangling her away from an onsite boyfriend when she was supposed to be working.

Josie's brows rose, her hands went to her chest in false innocence as she protested, "Not at all. I promise. Just a cute friend-y thing. You know how it is… like when you and Hayes used to work on the ranch together on breaks. Just some harmless flirting. I will not let my feelings get in the way of my work. I promise. I learned from the best—professional all the way!" Josie leapt in my arms, giving me another huge hug.

I held her at arm's length, looking her over. "Josie, if you're going to be a professional woman, you're going to need a new wardrobe. Let me take you shopping."

"Oh, goody! Let me just go throw on some jeans," she said, bouncing off to her room.

Despite my better judgement, I smiled. My little sister was finally growing up and committing to something. I just hoped I was strong enough to hold her accountable and help her succeed.

· · · · · · ·

My decision to hire my little sister was further tested on our shopping excursion. Everything I suggest Josie turned down as 'too stuffy, too loose, too old lady,' or 'too ugly.' I tried not to let my feelings get hurt—all the clothing I had suggested I would wear myself—and kept focused on our mission.

After buying cinnamon-sugar soft pretzels and lemonades to fortify ourselves, we found the perfect store, Charlie Rose. An elegant display of burgundy, pinks, and blacks greeted us, in young, chic cuts. It was the only store with clothing targeted at Josie's age that didn't look like it was suitable for working the pole at a bachelor party.

Holding one of the suits out to get a better look at it, I said, "Josie... I think our problem was your size. Everything was like a tent on you because you're so tiny." I handed her the suit jacket and skirt combo. "Look—no shoulder pads in this one."

She took the hanger in her hand. "Why do they put shoulder pads in women's suits, anyway? Why can't woman look business professional without looking like a man? Who wants to wear a suit at all? They were invented for and tailored for... men. Let's find something that screams, 'I'm a professional woman. With a vagina and tits and just because I'm pretty that doesn't mean I can't get the job done.'"

I laughed, telling her to keep her voice down. But, she was right. With Josie's feminist rant playing on repeat in my brain, I scanned the store. Ten department stores and two thousand calories later, I found it. Hanging above the racks, the perfect outfit was on display. Grabbing her arm, I breathed, "Josie. There!" and pointed across the room.

I drug her across the store. Signaling to the store clerk, I called, "Can you show us where that outfit is on the rack?"

A young clerk with a gorgeous smile said, "Certainly," and led us to a display in the back corner of the room.

I picked up the soft, buttery black leggings from the table. "Feel these, Josie. They are softer than those nasty sweatpants you wear." Glancing back up at the display, I confirmed, "You can be beautiful and comfortable." I picked up a long burgundy sleeveless tunic. The material flowed like water between my hands. With the black leggings and a pair of strappy metallic heels, Josie would still have her sexy punky edge, but fit right in working a wedding. "This top is gorgeous. And long enough to cover up that pert little ass of yours. I love this color for you," I said, holding it next to her face.

"But it's sleeveless. It will show my tattoos. Don't you think I have to cover them up to be professional?" she asked with a wince.

Josie's tattoos were a part of her story. Like a roadmap of her life up to this point. Why cover up who she was? "No. I don't. I want Josie Dixon on my staff. Her true self. Just dressed nicer. And... maybe brush that hair."

In classic Josie fashion, she stuck her tongue out at me. Then hugged me and whispered in my ear, "You are the best big sister in the world, you know that?"

• • • • • • •

Weeks went by and true to her word, Josie was everything I needed in an assistant. I couldn't have asked for a better employee. When I showed her how to lay out the flatware, or hang ribbons, her brown eyes focused on the task. Her little pearly white teeth would bite into the flesh of her lower lip. She would nod, murmuring, "Uh huh, uh huh." Then, she would take whatever I was working with out of my hands and repeat the action beautifully.

She was the perfect assistant.

There was just one hiccup. Colton.

About three weeks into Josie's trial period, Josie had a bad day. We were setting up Mess Hall for an Equestrian Brunch—horse enthusiasts were very particular, and everything had to be perfect. I was busy hanging horseshoes I had painted with a glossy white shellac. Josie was decorating six round tables for the event. Josie was quiet—which is extremely unusual for her. Tasks took her twice as long as normal. When I stopped to ask her if she was okay, I saw tears brimming in her eyes.

"He has a girlfriend. He brought her on my ranch." she wailed, throwing down the burlap ribbon she had been winding around the darling little silver glass horses I had bought for the occasion. (They had cost a pretty penny, but I would reuse them for a little girl birthday party the following week.)

"Ah, well, technically, this is Colton's ranch, honey," I said, only half listening as I tied the final shoe from the false beam I had Hayes put in when he first came back on the ranch. I did so love to have décor hanging above the guests.

She slumped down in one of the padded white folding chairs. Taking a horse in her hands, she twirled in under the light, mumbling, "But did he have to bring her here?"

We did not have time for this. We especially did not have time to be wiping her fingerprints off my ponies. I gently took the horse from her hand, rubbing with a spare cloth napkin. I put him back in his place on the table and picked up the burlap. Unwinding it from its cardboard spool, I asked, "Well, did you tell him how you feel about him?"

"Yes. That's what is even more humiliating. He said, he said, he said… I was like a sister to him! That's worse than him saying he didn't like me at all!" She threw her head back, covering her face with her hands.

"How is that worse?" I asked. I stood back to eye the

tables. I gave a nod of approval—burlap, silver, and white were the perfect color combination for today.

She sniffed. "Because it means he will never see me as anything other than a pesky little sister!"

Recently, I had seen the way Colton looked at Josie, and it was not with a chaste, brotherly eye. His gaze lingered on her longer than it should. He smiled while watching her from across the room. She had a tight little body and his eyes openly admired it. Beyond lust, I had no idea if Colton had deeper feelings for Josie. "Maybe he just cares about you too much to risk messing up what the two of you have. You guys have always been close friends."

"I'd be fine with that," she replied. "Kind of. But why bring this skanky—"

"Josie." I had to nip this in the bud. We had twenty women showing up in less than an hour. And it is never classy to call another woman a derogatory name.

"Okay, okay—but why bring this... *random*... onto my ranch and flaunt her in front of my face! It's uncalled for."

"I think we covered the fact that this is not your ranch, sweetie. And explain this to me... how is he flaunting her?" I asked, sneaking a look at the time on my phone.

Josie looked at me as if she was announcing a death sentence. "She comes for private riding lessons."

"Wait—she's taking lessons from him? How did you hear they were dating?" I asked.

She looked up at me sheepishly. "I didn't. But I just know. The way she looks at him with her stupid doe eyes. And you should see how many times a lesson she touches him. She always—"

I held my hand out to her. This had to stop. We needed to get back to work. And Josie needed to learn to behave professionally, no matter what her heart was telling her. "I'm going to stop you right there. As your boss, I am telling you right now that during your work day, your eyes need to be on your job. Not spying on Colton's lessons. You got that?"

She sighed in a way that told me she had been spying and she knew that I was right. "Yes."

"And stop jumping to conclusions, for goodness' sake," I said.

Josie stood, gathering the supplies from the table and putting them away in my rubber bin marked 'Horse Parties.' When she spoke, she was calmer and her voice was soft. "But he walked her to her car the other day. You tell me that isn't dating."

My heart went out to her. I'd be crushed if Hayes walked another woman out to her car. But I was also Josie's boss and it was my job to teach her—despite her feelings—to be professional. I wrapped my arm around her shoulder. "Honey, I know it's hard. But we work in a very close environment with the men we like, and we have to be—"

"If you say the 'p' word, my head is going to explode, Louie! I swear I cannot hear that word one more—

"Pussy?" I asked, trying to hold a straight face.

My sister's wide eyes snapped up to mine in shock. "Louanne Dixon, did you just say what I think you said?"

Her face was priceless. I laughed until my sides hurt. "See... I'm loosening up. I finally said the 'p' word."

She laughed along beside me. As we sat together, my arm around my wounded sister, my mind changed. Hayes and I were so happy together. What if I hadn't been so fearful of dating him? Could we have been happy together, sooner? And why shouldn't my sister go for Colton? She was busting her ass on the ranch and doing a fantastic job. Until this moment, she had shown no sign of weakness in struggling with these emotions at work.

And I had seen the way Colton looked at Josie. It was the same way Hayes looked at me. Sometime the big sister boss has to be the bossy big sister.

"Fuck it, Josie. Use that pussy. Wait—I mean... don't have sex or anything, but what the heck? Let Colton know how you feel. Make him realize that even though he cares for you as *much* as a sister, you are the furthest thing from it.

Show him you are a smart, sexy single woman—with a readily available, very non-sisterly pussy—who he would be lucky to get to date," I said.

Josie's wide eyes turned up at me, her mouth hung open. "Who are you and what did you do with my sister? And you can stop dropping the f-bomb and saying pussy now. Really. It sounds so unnatural coming from you." She shook her head in such a disgusted way, I laughed.

• • • • • • •

One week later, it was the end of Josie's trial month. She had done a fantastic job. The way she most impressed me was with how she was handling the Colton situation. Just a few hours after the Equestrian Brunch, she came to me and apologized for her emotional display during work hours. Then, she told me that she was here to work and that she wasn't going to let anything get in the way of her opportunity at having a career on the ranch. After our chat, I didn't see her give Colton much more than a polite 'hello.'

Josie brought a fun, light addition to the team. Her eye for detail improved with every event. By the end of her month, I happily told Hayes that he was completely right in telling me that I needed full-time help. And he agreed I had been right to take a chance on Josie. When it was time to tell my sister that she had earned the job, Hayes and I called her into my office. She tiptoed nervously through the door and quietly took a seat in one of the club chairs. Folding her hands demurely in her lap, she waited for us to speak.

The big sister in me couldn't help but make her sweat— just a little. Standing in front of her, I leaned back on my desk. Crossing my arms over my chest, I heaved a great sigh. "Josie, Josie, Josie. What are we going to do with you?"

Hayes took a seat in the club chair next to her. He held his hand over his mouth, hiding a grin.

Josie looked from me to Hayes, then back at me. "What? What did I do wrong?"

"Stealing," I said, narrowing my brow and trying to keep a straight face.

She popped up out of her chair like a jack in the box. "What? That's ridiculous."

Hayes stood as well. "I'm afraid we are going to have to have you escorted from the ranch. Memaw, can you come in here?" he called.

Josie's brows knit together in confusion as she looked to the doorway of my office. Memaw came in, carrying a crystal tray holding one of her famous triple chocolate cakes. The very same Brody had her make for me the day he gave me my full-time job.

Josie's hands went to her mouth, her eyes wide as she watched the entire staff of the ranch come in behind Memaw.

Brody gave her a big bear hug, saying, "Congratulations, kid, the job is yours."

They all hugged her and congratulated her. Then, Memaw suggested we move this party out of my tiny office and into the Mess Hall.

Josie lagged behind the others to hug me. "You mean it, Louie? You really want me?"

"Yes, Josie. You did a fantastic job. And you proved that when times get tough, you keep your emotions at bay and remain—"

"Don't say it!" she laughed.

"I'm going to say it. Professional." I gave her a kiss on the cheek. "Now let's go get some cake."

# CHAPTER EIGHT

Alice's face popped into the frame of my open office door. Her brow furrowed in confusion as she spoke. Her voice lilted at the end as if asking a question. "Louanne. You have a visitor?"

The local flower shop wasn't due to meet with me until two. I wasn't expecting anyone. Standing, I smoothed my skirt. I asked Alice, "Who is it?"

Before she could answer, a large woman dressed head to toe in a brightly colored floral pattern that hurt my eyes elbowed her way past Alice and into my office. A purple hat nearly tipped off her head as she struggled to get her large alligator skin purse and many bags through the door. Throwing her things down in one of my buffalo-checked club chairs, she plopped down in the other. Holding her hand up toward me, she said, "Pamela Greenwich. Pleased to make your acquaintance."

"Hello, Pamela." Hesitantly, I held my hand out to her. Taking it, she pumped it up and down several times, her grip digging into my bones. "I'm—

"Oh, honey! No need to introduce yourself! Louanne Dixon. Or, better known where I come from as, the queen of Ranch Romance." She reached up, straightening the brim of her hat.

"Ranch Romance?" I slowly eased myself down into my chair. "Excuse me? I'm not sure I know what you are talking about."

"Honey—have you not checked the hits on your website? Every time you post another event, every woman under the age of forty is clicking on it so fast your head would spin. I'm surprised you haven't cashed in, sold ads, and bought yourself a sweet little Porsche by now." Her eyes roved around my decorated office. "This is beautiful." Reaching into her bag, she pulled her phone and a pair of glasses out. Putting the glasses on the tip of her nose, she mumbled to herself, "Where is that tiny little picture of a camera?"

"Uh... ma'am," I said, trying to get the woman's attention.

"Hang on, honey. I just need to find this camera function, so I can start snapping pictures of your office. Why do they make the pictures so dang small?"

"I don't want to be rude, but you will most certainly not be photographing my office. I don't even know who you are!" I cried.

She looked up at me, her eyes wide with surprise. "How rude of me. Have I not properly introduced myself? Pamela Greenwich, queen of the blogging world. Ten years ago, I held the first bloggers conference for woman business owners—*Women Bloggers World*. Over one thousand women came. Today, ten thousand are in attendance. I'm surprised you haven't heard of me."

"I'm not online that much—other than Pinterest and posting on the site. And I wouldn't know the first thing about blogging."

"Honey—you are already a famous blogger. I may be behind on the technology—my assistants handle the majority of the tech stuff—but you have to tell me you realize that those pretty pics and comments you post on the CLAS website are considered a blog. Women wait on pins and needles by their computers to see your latest events. I assume you've been booked every weekend for the next year?"

"Well, yes, but that's just because Brody's been growing the business. CLAS ranch did happen to make it to *Travel and Dining*'s Top Ten destination weddings. Is that how you heard of me? Through the Top Ten article?" I asked.

"*Travel and Dining*? What on Earth is that? No. It's because of your blog. Don't the clients mention it to you when they book the place?" she asked.

I did get a lot of compliments about the posts I did on the website from potential clients. Now that Pamela mentioned it, looking back over the past six months, every bride who had come in had, in some way, mentioned the site. I breathed, "I had no idea."

"Have you ever checked your analytics? Saw how many hits you were getting?" she asked.

Wordlessly, I shook my head. "I would have no idea how to even go about that."

Pamela called over her shoulder. "Derrick! Bring the laptop!" She gave me a broad smile.

I watched in shock as a thin, tall man in a too small black suit came scurrying into my office. Giving me an apologetic nod as way of introduction, he placed the open laptop he held in his hand onto my desk. "Miss Louanne, it's a pleasure to meet you in the flesh. Can I just say that you have absolutely turned New York society on its head with your Ranch Romance designs? For the first time in the history of brides, we are seeing women tromp down the aisle in the cowgirl boot."

"Uh, thanks?" I replied. My eyes focused on the page he had up on his computer. It was an analysis of CLAS ranch's monthly website visits. My brow knitted together. "How did you get this information? Isn't it private?"

A blush rose on Derrick's cheeks. He breathed the word with reverence. "Hayes."

Pamela fanned her face with her hand. "My, my, my, you

all grow them up right out here in the middle of nowhere. Where are we again, Derrick?"

"Wyoming," he answered.

"Whew. Well, I do say whatever you are feeding these cowboys is doing them right. I've never seen such strapping young men in my life—no offense, Derrick—"

"None taken, Ms. Pam."

"And that Hayes, what a—"

"He's mine, Ms. Pamela," I said.

"I already knew that, Louanne. You should hear the way he talks about you. I wouldn't be surprised if he's asking you to marry him before the year is up," she hooted.

"He *has* asked me to marry him. We are engaged." I held my ring out for Pamela and Derrick's inspection.

"Gosh almighty, girl—that rock is big enough to ice skate on! Not only did you catch yourself one hunk'a burning love, looks like the cowboy is loaded to boot. Did I just make a pun? Derrick, was that a pun?"

Derrick cleared his throat. "It's a lovely ring, Ms. Louanne. And you will make a lovely bride."

"How are your wedding plans going, Louanne? A wedding planner like you? Well now, that's going to be the most perfect, beautiful wedding ever. You are going to put all the other weddings to shame, girl. I just know it. What are your colors going to be?" She sat on the edge of her seat awaiting my reply.

"I… ah… I'm not sure yet," I answered.

"Well, what about decorations? Are you going to go with your more rustic, woodsy themes, or really play up that ranch romance you are so well known for?" She looked at me expectantly.

"I… I'm not sure," I answered.

"How about the cake? That's an easy one. Chocolate or vanilla?"

I had no idea why, but her questions had me near tears. My cheeks flushed, and an uneasy feeling crept into my stomach. My answer came out in a rush of breath. "I don't know."

Derrick smiled at me sympathetically. I had a feeling Pamela probably overwhelmed him from time to time as well. "I'm sure it will be a lovely occasion. Perhaps we should get back to the numbers? Ms. Louanne, here is the number of visits your website has had in the past year—"

I interrupted, "It's not my website. It's Brody's. He owns the ranch. He started it years ago. Then, when I went full time, he added a section for me to post about the weddings."

"And the section he added to the website is called a blog, Miss Louanne," Derrick said respectfully.

I rubbed my forehead with my hand. "Well, I get that, but I was never 'blogging.' I was just updating our website after events—"

Derrick softened his voice. "I understand. But the only page people are visiting is the one that you manage. And your following is increasing daily. If you created your own wedding/ event blog, with these very same posts, you would have a very substantial income. Very." His brows rose to me as if to reiterate the word *very*.

I stood from my chair, saying, "I'm sorry—this is all just a bit much for me. I wasn't expecting company, and I don't know much about website analysis, and... where did you say you were from?"

"New York City. We just got in this morning. We like to surprise our next victim," Pamela said with a big grin.

"Victim?" I asked, feeling my face pale.

Derrick shot a 'behave already' look Pamela's way. "What Ms. Greenwich means to say is that we like to come unannounced. That way the media and bigger corporations don't get wind of who our next blogging star is before we can interact with them. You stand to make a lot more money if we help you instead of them. And all we ask is that you speak at Women's Blogger World in exchange for our services."

I held up my hands. "I appreciate your coming all this

way, but—"

Pamela interrupted before I could continue. "Say no more. It's a lot to think about and Derrick has a ton to go over with you before you make your decision. Don't give us an answer yet. Let's share a meal and then when you have a full stomach we can hit the books. Memaw invited us to lunch, didn't she, Derrick?"

He shot me another apologetic look. "She did. Ribs, I think she said?"

Standing up from her chair, Pamela took her glasses off, folding them carefully and handing them to Derrick. He took them from her and slid them into his breast pocket. Pamela put both her hands on my desk, leaning in. Her face became stoic. Her demeanor reminded me of old mafia movies as she spoke. "Blogging is a very, very lucrative business."

Derrick shot me a look. "Very."

"What exactly does 'very' mean to you?" I asked.

"Our least paid blogger clears about three grand a month," he answered.

Pamela boasted, "But our highest paid friend makes over three times that. And they have plenty of time to keep their full-time job, too. Not to mention the sponsorships, payment for trial products, speaking engagements. It's a very lucrative career."

Quickly, I did the math in my head. Even if I averaged less than their highest paid blogger, if I kept my job at the ranch and started my own site for the events, I would double my salary. "But then my clients would be faced with ads every time they wanted to see pictures from an event?"

Pamela dismissed my concern with a wave of her hand in the air. "People are immune to ads. They don't even see them these days. But we'll cover all that with you. First, let's go dig into those ribs. I can't wait to try some good old-fashioned country cooking." Leaving her bags in my chair, Pamela showed herself out of my office.

Giving me another apologetic smile, Derrick closed the

laptop, thrust it underneath his arm, and followed his boss through the door.

Heaving a great sigh, I flopped down into my chair. Ten minutes with those two strangers and I was completely wiped out. Picking up my notebook, I looked over my to-do list for the day. I could just forget about it. From what I had gleaned of Pamela, she was going to steamroll any plans I had made for my day.

I wanted to hide in my office. But, I was hungry. And I wanted to see Hayes. Also, to ask him what he was thinking when he gave access to the website to these crazy New Yorkers.

Entering the Mess Hall, I heard Pamela before I saw her. Her booming voice carried through the hall. "And Memaw, you could debut your recipes on the site. A whole downhome cooking blog to accompany the wedding one. Louanne could take the photographs of the food—does she do all her own photography, because it's phenomenal—and…"

Her voice prattled on as I tried to make my way through the shadows to find Hayes. Where was he? My stomach rumbled, my hunger suddenly overtaking my desire to find my man. I managed to sneak into the double doors of the kitchen.

Memaw was standing at the stove, serving up huge plates of ribs, mashed potatoes, and buttery ears of corn. When she saw me, she hollered out, "There's the lady of the hour! That Pamela had been asking for your whereabouts. I told Hayes she was going to be too much for you and you'd be hiding out. Here you go—eat up. I think you're going to need your strength to deal with those two." With a loud cackle, she handed me a plate.

"Thanks. I think I'll just eat in here if you don't mind." I pulled up a stool to her counter and dug my fork into the pile of creamy potatoes.

"I'll let Hayes know you're in here, sweetheart," she said with a nod.

I gave her a grateful smile. "Thanks—"

Memaw hollered over her shoulder at the office door behind her. "Haaaayes!"

I laughed, taking another bite of my potatoes. Looking up, my heart skipped a little beat as Hayes appeared in the kitchen. He took a plate from Memaw, giving her a kiss on the cheek. He pulled up a stool, sitting down next to me and kissing my cheek as well.

"Thanks for lunch, Memaw," he said, spreading a napkin in his lap.

Memaw wiped her hands on her apron, giving Hayes a stern look. "I told you she'd be hiding out after you let those New Yorkers loose on her."

My brows rose to Hayes. "You care to explain what Pamela Greenwich and her sidekick are doing having access to CLAS' website?"

He shrugged, picking up a sauce-covered rib. "Pamela came to me this morning. She made some great points. I think she might be right."

"Right about what?" I asked.

He took a bite, dabbed at his mouth, then looked at me. "You, Louanne. When they came into my office and told me about how popular your posts have become, I grew curious. When I pulled up the website analytics, I was stunned. Your posts have incredibly heavy traffic. You stand to make a lot of money through advertising on your own site."

"And so, you just let them right into my office?" I asked.

He gave a chuckle. "I just pictured you sitting at your desk, that to-do list in front of you, tackling your day, and then, Pamela busting in with that hat on and everything. It was just too good of an opportunity to pass up. I apologize—I guess Colton's pranking ways have rubbed off on me."

"It was... quite a surprise, I have to say." I gave a laugh, remembering Pamela's grand entrance.

"I would have loved to see your face when she came into

your office," Hayes said.

"She certainly made herself comfortable," I replied.

"Oh, good—I told her she should," he said.

I laughed.

"Seriously though, Luna. This could be a good opportunity for you. They want you to speak at the bloggers conference in New York, even though you had no idea that you were running a blog. You'd be great. And if that many people like your style, you may as well meet them. Not to mention, the additional income you'd be earning, just by doing what you are already doing."

I felt sick. "But New York? I've never even left the state of Wyoming. And speaking in front of hundreds of women—"

"Thousands, actually," he added.

"I can't even wrap my head around it. And being gone from the ranch. I don't think I want to do that."

"You've worked your entire teen and adult life on this. Why not see where it could go?" he asked.

Another woman might jump on the opportunity to go to New York City, become a fancy blogger, double their income. But I was happy here. And I had a wedding to plan. Also, I rarely left Little Peak, much less the ranch. The idea of getting on a plane and flying to a conference to speak to women... it turned my stomach.

"I don't think it's such a good idea—"

"There she is! The queen of Ranch Romance herself!"

I cringed as Pamela and Derrick made their way into the kitchen.

Pamela put her hand over her belly. "Memaw—I have to hand it to you. That meal beat our delis any day. We really must talk about a food blog for you."

Hayes laughed as I slouched down beside him. He whispered into my ear, "Just hear her out, Luna. Then, we can send them on their way with a doggie bag of ribs."

I knew I should be flattered at the least. Maybe even excited by the opportunity. But all I could think about was that plane ride to a strange city I had never been to. And the faces of all those women, expecting me to say something brilliant.

What could I say? I just liked things to be organized. And pretty. How does one turn that into a bloggers workshop for thousands of people?

•••••••

"You have to go to New York, Louanne! You just have to!" Georgia sat on my desk, her long legs folded over one another. The second Pamela and Derrick left, she pounced on me, wanting the scoop about the two strangers who had visited me. "If you don't go, I'm going to go and pretend I'm you, just for the free trip! When I lived in Idaho, our high school class went there for our senior trip and it was awesome. And that was only getting to see the boring stuff, like the museums. Think about all the cool bars and restaurants you could go to."

Though Pamela had promised the trip of a lifetime, the idea of braving the conference still turned my stomach. "Trust me, Georgia. If I could send you in my place, I would. Big cities and crowds are not my thing."

Georgia stared at me in disbelief. "How do you know? You've never been anywhere bigger than Jackson!"

I heaved a sigh. "I just know, okay? I know myself. I'm just boring old Louanne Dixon. Born and raised right here in Little Peak and perfectly happy—"

Josie burst into my office, her eyes wide as saucers. "Shut up! We are going to New York! Oh, my God, I'm so excited—Colton just told me about the bloggers conference and I can't wait. I have to decide what tattoo I'm going to get while we're there." She plopped herself down in the club chair Pamela had helped herself to just hours before.

"There is no 'we,' Josie. I'm not even sure if I'm going to go, yet. But I am sure about one thing and that is the invitation was not extended to the entire ranch," I said.

"But I'm your assistant," she pouted. "I have to come."

"I don't think Pamela is going to be springing for first-class air fare, all paid meals, and a five-star hotel for two people, Josie," Georgia said.

My sister was going to kill me when I added to the fact she would not be coming to the trip. "Well... actually. Pamela did offer to pay for two airfares and meal allowances. But the other ticket would be for... Hayes."

Josie's mouth opened in shock. Then, she wailed, "What? Why?"

A new voice to the discussion chimed in with her opinion. "She probably knew Louanne would never leave the ranch without that, and I'm quoting, 'hunk of a cowboy' by her side." I looked up to see Bridgette standing in the doorframe, her arms crossed over her chest. "Am I right, Louanne?"

Georgia had a glimmer in her eye as she countered with, "Or maybe Pamela knew Hayes would never let Louanne off Wyoming soil without him by her side. Is that what happened, Louanne?"

I thought back to the discussion between Hayes, Pamela, and me. When Pamela said, "It would be best if Louanne came alone so she has fewer... distractions," I believe Hayes' exact words were, "Oh, hell, no. That's just not the way things are down here on the ranch, Ms. Greenwich. A young lady traveling to a big city requires a male escort to ensure her safety." I looked at Georgia. "We have a winner." I quickly added, "Not that I wouldn't have gone on my own, if I wanted to that is."

Three pairs of doubtful female eyes stared back at me.

"I'm surprised he letting you go at all," Bridgette said.

"There is no 'letting' me. Besides, it was his idea. I didn't even want to go in the first place. Hayes is worried down the road I might regret having let the opportunity pass me by. But yes, if I go, he will come with me. Which is what I want."

Josie threw me another pouty face. "But we'd have so

much fun together, Louie. Let me come and be your escort!"

"I think your escorting is exactly what Hayes is afraid of," Georgia mumbled, grinning.

"I resent that comment," Josie sniffed at Georgia.

Looking Josie's way, Bridgette said, "I think you meant 'resemble' that comment. The last time we went to Jackson, wasn't it you that got all the girls up and dancing on the bar?"

"Yeah—and I'm the one who got in trouble for it," Georgia said, shooting Josie a dirty look.

Bridgette wiggled her brows. "Not me. Travis found it to be very sexy."

I gave a loud groan, putting my head on my desk. "Can't you all just get out of here? With all this New York talk, I haven't gotten a single thing done." Lifting my head, I placed my face into my hands, begging the girls with my gaze to shoo.

Ignoring my face, Bridgette took a seat in the chair next to Josie. "I for one think Louanne should stay. I mean, who wants to cash in on their fame, get a free trip—"

Georgia interrupted, "With first-class airfare."

Bridgette continued, "With first-class airfare, and money to blow on the best food. Then, back at the hotel, a hot cowboy in between your thousand count thread sheets, and room service. Then the giants of the blogging community showing you how to turn your pretty pictures into dollar signs."

Josie rolled her eyes. "Yeah. Who would want that?"

There was knock on the door. We all looked over to find Brody and Hayes standing in the doorway. The way they were chuckling made it obvious they'd overheard our little convo.

Brody spoke first. "Ladies, sorry to interrupt, but we have some good news."

"Derrick is not only straight, he's single?" Josie asked cheekily.

"I think Derrick likes cowboys as much as you do, Josie," Brody said with a laugh. "But you can find out for sure when we fly to New York to meet up with him."

My little sister's jaw dropped open. "What? I get to go?"

Hayes said, "Pamela said that as a woman she just couldn't pass up the opportunity of funding a 'girls gone wild' trip. So, she offered to pay for all four of you ladies to go."

Josie hopped up from her seat, dancing around, chanting, "Girls' trip, girls' trip!"

Georgia eyed Brody suspiciously. "What's the catch?"

"Hayes and I will be joining you as escorts," Brody answered.

"More like bodyguards," Bridgette laughed.

Brody put his hands up. "Look at it however you want to, but we know you ladies would be fine on your own. You are all strong, independent women. But as Jenkins men, we can't help but to feel a little better accompanying you. We promise we won't cramp your style."

"Unless you get yourselves into trouble. Then, we will most definitely be cramping your style," Hayes added sternly.

Josie tried to look casual as she asked, "Is Travis coming? Oh, and what about... Colton? Is he coming as well?"

Brody tried to hide his smile. "Travis said he wanted to stay here with Lila Bell and that Bridgette deserves a girls' trip." He raised a teasing brow to Bridgette. "And that I can spank her ass if she gets out of line. Colton offered to stay behind and watch the ranch for us."

Hayes' gaze landed on mine. "But it's all up to Louanne. Luna, you can say no to this if you want to. The trip, the speaking engagement, if it's not something you want to do, just tell us. The girls will understand."

A fully paid first-class trip to New York City with my fiancé and best girlfriends. Who wouldn't want that? Boring old plain Jane, never been out of the state, Louanne Dixon.

SHANNA HANDEL

That's who. I looked over the faces of the girls. My sister was shooting me 'I will kill you if you say no' looks. Georgia was looking at me with her big green Bambi eyes. Bridgette was smiling broadly, already knowing my answer. There was no way out. Even if I wanted one. They would badger me until I conceded. Heaving a sigh, I said, "I'm going to need an audience to practice on. Pamela said I have a full forty-five minutes to fill."

A joint squeal erupted in my office. We were going to New York.

• • • • • • •

"Ever heard of the mile-high club?" Hayes squeezed my thigh, his eyes looking blue as he raised a saucy brow at me.

The idea of any part of my body making contact with that tiny, filthy toilet gave me a shudder. "You have to be joking. There is nothing sexy about doing... *it*... in a nasty airplane bathroom. Besides, did you get a look at the guy that just walked out of there holding a newspaper? No, thank you."

Hayes gave a chuckle. "Good point. Let's save it for the five-star hotel."

I held out my 2.3-carat diamond, joking in a snobby tone, "Three thousand count thread sheets—that's so much more my style."

He leaned over, whispering in my ear, "Like I haven't had you on the floor of the barn on a pile of hay?" My pussy clenched at his words, my nose filling with the soft, sweet smell of hay. "And in the bed of my truck. And in the changing rooms at the lake. You dirty girl, you'd do it anywhere I said if I just touch you." Throwing the thin blue felt airplane blanket over my lap, his fingers wandered toward my pussy. I leaned my head back on the headrest of the plush leather seat.

Hayes leaned back as well, closing his eyes as if he were asleep. He murmured to me, "There is more than one way

158

to become a member of the club." I closed my eyes as well, feigning sleep, should a stewardess walk by. His hand slipped underneath my skirt, cupping my pussy. My head lolled back.

His fingers found their way into my panties. He dipped into my folds, collecting my juices. Then, he began rubbing my clit, softly at first. Then harder and faster. He spoke as he rubbed. "Remember that time in the barn? When you were being naughty and teasing me?" I nodded my head slightly, holding in a moan.

"I took you over my knee and spanked your bottom a pretty pink. You liked that, didn't you, you naughty tease? Little girls that tease Daddy get their asses spanked." My hips moved discreetly underneath the blanket as he continued to rub. My pussy clenched, a fresh wetness drenching my panties. "Then I bent you over the hay bales, flipped your skirt up over your back, and fucked you from behind. Remember that? Your pussy was so tight, and you were screaming. I pulled your hair and slapped your ass. You loved every minute of it, didn't you, you dirty girl?"

"Uh-huh," I moaned quietly as he stroked. My pussy tightened, and I came in a quick bursting rush. "That was my kind of mile-high club," I whispered. Shuddering, I lay my head on his shoulder. He wrapped his arm around me, chuckling as I fell asleep.

• • • • • • •

We were all thrilled when we reached the hotel. Exhausted from the day's travels, I lay on the crisp white sheets of the bed.

"You only have a few minutes to rest. We're meeting the others for dinner," Hayes said, walking about the room as he unpacked our luggage.

I moaned. "But I'm tired and you know how I get when I'm tired. Grumpy."

"And you know what happens when you get grumpy.

Spanked," Hayes replied as he hung his white button-down shirt up in the closet.

I was beyond tired. But also, I was incredibly nervous. I lay on the bed, hating that I felt so on edge when I should be enjoying this trip with the man of my dreams and my closest friends. What I really wanted was to crawl into my bed at home underneath my piles of comforters and have Daddy tuck me in.

The hour of rest time went by too fast. Dressing for dinner, I lacked my usual care for hair and makeup. Hayes wrapped his arms around me, kissing me and fussing over me. When he asked me what was wrong, I brushed him off and told him I was fine.

The meal was plated beautifully, the décor and lighting in the restaurant elegant. I should have been enjoying myself, or at least gathering ideas for my next black-tie event, but instead, I moodily pushed food around on my plate. Only Hayes could sense my unhappiness; he kept one arm around me the entire meal. The girls were excited to be at a fancy New York eatery, and the three of them kept up the chatter, too excited to notice how quiet I was.

The conversation eventually turned to me and the speech I would be giving the next day. I tried to change the subject few times, but they persisted until I could stand it no longer. Out of nowhere, and completely out of character for me, I shouted, "Can we please stop talking about the damn speech?" Hayes quietly excused us from the table, pleading fatigue and escorted me from the table.

During the taxi ride back, I knew I was in trouble. An uneasy feeling came over me as I sat back in my seat, arms crossed over my chest. Once we were alone in the room, Hayes gathered me onto his lap.

"Baby girl, this is a once in a lifetime trip. You are miserable. This is so unlike you. What is going on?" he asked, stroking my hair.

I put my head in my hands. "It's so stressful. Public speaking is collectively the human race's greatest fear and here I am preparing to go on stage and talk to hundreds of women! Don't I get a free pass to be a bitch this one night? Cut me a break." I pushed myself up and out of his lap.

His hand wrapped around my waist, tugging me back down onto his lap. His face was inches from mine. His tone was low and laced with anger. "You are my woman and so that excludes you from having a pass to speak to people the way you spoke to them tonight. Ever."

I froze. Words lodged in my throat. I couldn't speak. My gaze locked with his, his eyes flashed.

I gulped.

"Tonight, we are going to have a little chat. Tomorrow, you are going to find everyone and apologize to them for your behavior and thank them for coming on this trip with you," he said.

"Yes, Daddy," I whispered. Ice formed in my stomach as my buttocks clenched. When a daddy says 'little chat,' it means one thing… spanking.

"Good girl. Looks like someone needs a little stress relief spanking," he said.

My eyebrows shot up. We had covered the 'sexy make you dripping wet' spanking, and the 'you've been a bad girl and are going to spend the rest of the day standing' spanking, but a stress relief spanking was something I had never heard of. "What's that?"

"It's somewhere between a playful spanking and a punishment spanking. It's for baby girls that need a release. It will help you let go, relax. And, as your daddy I will get the satisfaction of spanking your ass for the way you were acting tonight."

It sounded like exactly what I needed after the traveling and with the pressure of the big speech on my mind. I sniffed, "Sorry, Daddy."

"I know you are, sweetheart. Undress and lie over my lap," he demanded.

I stood up, my hands trembling as I removed my shirt. My bra was next. I was embarrassed by how hard my nipples were from the prospect of my spanking. I took down my skirt and panties. Standing before him, naked, I blushed as his eyes traveled over my body.

"Over you go," he said, patting his thighs. I carefully crawled over his legs. My upper body rested comfortably on the bed. My legs spread out straight on top of the bed. My bare bottom was perfectly centered over his lap. His hand rested on my ass as he spoke. "You are under an intense amount of pressure. But that's no excuse for your behavior, is it, young lady?"

"No, Daddy," I murmured. His hand came down on the center of my right cheek in a hard smack that echoed through the room. My ass jiggled, the sting spreading. My pussy was already getting wet—how I loved the feeling of being nude and lying over his lap while he was fully dressed and in complete control of me. It made me feel vulnerable and safe and chastised all at once. It was a feeling I had longed for all my life, but had never known I was missing.

He spanked my bottom again. "You are going to do your best tomorrow and that is all you can do. Let everything else go," he said.

"Yes, Daddy," I said. The next spank landed on the center of my left cheek. My ass jiggled again, that cheek now stinging with a matching warmth.

"And you are going to be a good girl on this trip and be nice to your friends." he said, spanking as he lectured. My bottom was warming from the stinging spanks and my hips started to wiggle. "Because if you talk to Daddy like that again, I'm afraid I'll have to punish you no matter who is watching. Do you want to be the naughty little girl who goes over Daddy's knee and has her panties pulled down, her bottom spanked for all to see?"

"Oh, no, Daddy!" A shiver ran through me at the thought. Would he really do that? What would people say? He was the most strict of the daddies. I could imagine there was a line with him that if it was crossed, he wouldn't think twice to spank me in public. The idea made my pussy pulse and gush.

He spanked the same spot on the right side, then the left side, then right, then the left again. My skin burned. I wiggled my hips in discomfort. I knew what he was waiting to hear. "I'll be good the rest of the trip. I promise, Daddy."

"That's my good girl. But I still want to help you relieve the stress. You know what else is good for relaxing?" he asked.

"No, Daddy. Tell me," I said.

"A good, hard fuck. Like the one I gave you in the barn that day," he said.

I moaned, remembering the day he spoke of. "I'm feeling less stressed already." Hayes lifted my hips, moving me off his lap and over the edge of the bed. Moments later he was behind me, the sound of his belt buckle making my nipples further harden. He rubbed his rock-hard cock against the entrance of my wet pussy. Pushing within me, a burning pain shot through my pussy. I moaned as he slid further in, his balls pressing against my ass as he gave me his full length.

He began pumping hard and fast, and I gathered the sheets in my hands as I screamed, "Oh, my God!" Each fuck was a hard, punishing invasion that made my pussy weep and tighten around his cock. I began making a strange mewing noise as I stood up on tiptoe, pushing my toes into the carpet and my breasts further into the mattress as I took what he gave me. "Unh, unh, unh," I cried as my hips lifted to meet his force-filled pumps.

He had only been inside me for a few moments, but between lying over his lap naked, his hand spanking my ass, and the way he had called himself my daddy and said I was naughty, and oh my, threatened to spank me in public, it was too much. Tears stung at my eyes as I locked around his cock and came with an explosion. My entire body went rigid as the waves of pleasure tore through my pussy. Then, I collapsed against the bed as he continued to fuck me to his own sweaty climax.

• • • • • • •

Later that night I lay in our hotel bed, staring at the ceiling. Our intense lovemaking session had taken away ninety percent of the stress I felt. But there was still that nagging ten percent, whispering in my ear about how many people would be watching me in the morning. And I absolutely hated the speech that I had written. I was not a blogger—I was a wedding planner. So how on Earth was I supposed to give a speech on writing a successful blog? As Hayes slept in the bed, I sat at the hotel desk, my pussy still sore, and chewed on the end of my pen.

Didn't someone famous once say, 'write what you know'?

Here was what I knew—how to plan a wedding, and how to make a list.

Pamela's advice was to begin to cater to wedding planners through my blog. She suggested that in addition to blogging about my events, I should write articles for my readers about the less pretty side of things—the working, moving pieces of wedding planning.

I was a little intimidated by the writing aspect of a real blog. In the past I had mostly posted pictures with descriptions on the site. I had decided to start with a simple piece—a list.

After all, Pamela had seen me scribbling furiously in my notebook and had asked to read them. I had shown her a few and she had loved them. And, can you ever go wrong with a Top Ten list?

Flipping over my computer, I scanned my latest blog post. Nerves danced in my stomach as I reread it, wondering what the readers thought of the change from my usual.

*Top Ten ways to make a bride's dreams come true, by Louanne Dixon*
1.    Always, always, always listen to your bride. You will

be surprised to know that you may be the only one in her life that is actually listening to her concerns, desires, and goals. Weddings often bring out the worst in family members and attention is placed on themselves and not the bride. Give her that support by being there for her during what is meant to be the most special event of her life, but what can also be the most stressful.

2. There is no such thing as a bridezilla. Just a poorly managed bride. If your bride is showing those 'zilla-like qualities, see point number one. Most likely she just needs to feel like someone listening to her.

3. Set the budget from the get-go, and stick with it. No one day is worth being in debt for the rest of your life. Make sure the bride knows how much she has to spend from day one, then stay with that number. Never, ever encourage said bride to blow said budget.

4. Find clever ways to save money on decorations. Thrift stores have gorgeous crystal platters and goblets for dollars. Do not underestimate your local dollar store. They often have higher end items in their party section that just happened to be overstock from more expensive stores. Offer to go in with the bride fifty-fifty if she lets you keep the décor. She's saving money and you'll have a fantastic stock of decorations for some of your tighter budgets.

5. Serve food the bride and groom actually like to eat. This is a tricky one because they will have every family member they know—including third cousins they've only met once—filling them in on their likes, dislikes, allergies, etc. I once had to feed a bride a granola bar straight out of my purse because there was nothing at her wedding she could eat. Boy, I learned my lesson after that one!

6. Don't forget to feed the bride and groom. Trust

me—they will be so busy talking and dancing and shaking hands, they may not get a chance to eat. Be sure to fix them each a plate and find a quiet moment for them to eat together. Of all the things you do for your bride, I guarantee this is the one that will be the most appreciated on the big day.

7. Double, triple, quadruple check your vendors. Do not leave it up to chance. I call all my vendors the day before the wedding as well as again on the big day to be sure they have the correct time and place. If they don't pick up, I double call. I've even been known to block my number, so they don't know it's me. I like to have my verbal commitment twice in the twenty-four-hour time.

8. Never, ever let a guest that is not part of the wedding party make a speech. Trust me on this one—listening to her uncle Larry tell all of her closest friends how the wart on his hand that refused to go away reminded him of the groom's persistence while courting his shapely niece is not how the bride wants to spend her big day.

9. Take the time to save mementos for her. Ask for a (clean) stack of paper napkins from the bakery that did the cake. Find a discarded bouquet of flowers and dry them for her. Keep the notes you took while planning and put them all in a pretty folder to give her after the wedding.

10. Take care of yourself. How can you be there for your bride on her big day if you aren't taking care of yourself? Go to bed early the night before. Eat a big breakfast—it's probably the only meal you'll get the day of the wedding. Throw some snacks in your purse. And take time to do your hair and look your best. A frazzled wedding planner is not going to give the bride the confidence she needs to feel in order to walk down that aisle.

It wasn't half bad. I read the list one more time. Sitting back in my chair, I contemplated. If I couldn't tell these women how to run their blog, I could at least share with them my knowledge about how to plan a wedding, and how to take care of a bride. It may not make them any money, but it's what I knew how to do. And every woman, at some point in her life, finds herself the one in charge of taking care of a bride. So at least I wouldn't be completely wasting their time.

I grabbed my notebook from my bag and started jotting down some talking points based on my list.

At seven o'clock the next morning I stood before a crowd of one thousand women and told them the top ten ways to make a bride's dreams come true. I received a standing ovation that warmed my heart. But it couldn't top the feeling I got from the look in Hayes' eyes when he came up to me, kissed me on the cheek, and said, "I'm so proud of you, baby girl."

During the rest of the day we blew off the conference. I was too strung out on adrenaline afterwards to sit still and listen to lectures. Instead, we explored New York with our friends. I took my first subway ride (I found being underground with hundreds of people disgusting and I wanted to take a shower afterwards) ate hotdogs in Central Park (made me miss Memaw's cooking and our sit-down lunches in the Mess Hall), and saw a Broadway show. I did enjoy the show.

Then, as one would expect when letting my little sister, carefree Georgia, and wild woman Bridgette go shopping in a big, classy city like New York, the girls got into trouble. Brody was very clear that we were always to stay together. He gave us a long lecture about being in a strange city and strength in numbers, etc., that came complete with 'the look' and 'the tone' that told us he meant business. After a few hours of shopping on Fifth Avenue, we were to meet back at the hotel lobby then we would all get ready for a late dinner out.

Well, that never happened.

Instead, we of course got split up from one another. As per my request, we started our outing at Bergdorf Goodman, a former Vanderbilt Mansion turned department store. Georgia was itching to get to the three-story Dolce & Gabbana and check out the leopard print mini-dresses while Bridgette had her heart set on spending money on the rock-stud gear at Valentino. Josie was just a ball of spastic energy, ready to hop from one store to the next.

With only a limited amount of time, we all agreed it would be best to split up, then meet back outside the hotel at seven forty-five p.m. What Brody had said made sense, but we women were on a mission. And how often does a group of girls in from the middle of nowhere Wyoming get to shop on Fifth Avenue?

Our plan was to stroll into the lobby to meet Brody and Hayes at eight o'clock, and the men would be none the wiser. With our glossy packages in hand, we would float up the elevators to dress for dinner in our rooms, then be off to make our reservations at The League of Kitchens. Nothing looks sillier than a group of grown women making a pinky promise outside the doors of one of the world's most famous department stores, but we did. Locking little fingers, we all swore we would be outside our hotel at the right time.

Fast forward to eight fifteen: I'd been patiently waiting outside the hotel since seven-thirty, with Georgia—who came flying toward me with her hair blowing behind her and more packages than a woman should be able to carry, at seven fifty-five—standing beside me in a brand new tiny dress. A very livid Brody and Hayes were flanking us like bodyguards.

Josie came tripping up the street, the heel of her broken patent leather shoe in one hand, a half-eaten soft pretzel in the other. Bridgette was running beside her, wearing a necklace that looked like a dog collar and holding a large plastic cup of what looked suspiciously like a margarita, and three giant shopping bags.

Josie and Bridgette were sent to their room and grounded from dinner. Brody marched Georgia off to their room, one hand wrapped firmly around her leopard-printed bottom as they exited. And Hayes took me upstairs for a good old-fashioned 'talking to.' His arm was around my shoulder, he carried my shopping bags in his hand. My tummy did flip-flops as the elevator rose to our floor. I could feel him tense beside me, the anger practically radiating off his body. Without looking over at his profile, I knew that little muscle in his jaw was jumping. Daddy was not happy.

We both stared forward at the elevator doors. A quiet 'ding' announced our arrival. As the doors opened, Hayes leaned down, his breath hot in my ear. "Having to be punished twice in one trip? I have a solution for unruly behavior. You know what it is?"

Biting my lip, I shook my head. A shiver ran down my spine as I murmured, "Uh-uh."

"My cock in your ass." He grabbed my arm, leading me from the elevator to our room. My jaw dropped to my chest, my bottom clenching as I walked. He unlocked our door.

"W-what?"

"You heard me." Tossing the bags on the chair, he locked the door. "Take off all your clothes."

Knots formed in my stomach. Chill bumps rose on my arms. I stared at his face. His gray eyes flashed, his jaw tightening as he waited. Quickly, I slipped off my heels. The dress was easy enough to remove. I pulled it up and over my head and stood before him in nothing but my bra and panties.

He crossed his arms over his chest. "Don't make me wait."

My pussy gushed at the sight of his lifted brow. My fingers fumbled with the hooks of my bra, eventually freeing my breasts. My nipples were already pebbled from his commanding tone. I slipped my panties down, kicking them from my foot onto the floor.

Hayes' eyes roved over me hungrily. He sat on the edge of the bed and patted his lap. "Come lie over me."

Giving him one long, pleading look, I tiptoed toward him. Grabbing my hips, he guided me into place so that I was over his lap as he would if he were going to spank me. "Relax your muscles," he said. His hand began lightly stroking my bare back. Goosebumps rose on my skin as I unclenched my muscles. "Spread your legs."

Shame pulsed through my being as I spread my legs over his lap. I took a deep breath, closing my eyes and pressing my cheek into the back of my hands on the bed. His finger slipped into my pussy. I gasped at his touch, my pussy quivering as his finger made its entrance, swirling and collecting my juices. His finger left my pussy, sliding up my perineum. I wanted to clench my bottom but I resisted. He touched my rosebud and my eyes squeezed shut tighter. I couldn't believe this was happening! No one had ever been near this place of my body. Nor had it ever crossed my mind that a lover would show interest in it. My head spun as his fingertip, slick with my juices, explored my quivering entrance. My nipples tightened, my pussy clenched as he slipped into my bottom. "Relax. Embrace the sensation."

Breathing deeply, I allowed my body to respond to his intrusion. There was a stinging pain as a second finger pushed past my tight entrance. The inside of my bottom stretched and I gasped as his fingers moved inside of me. I felt out of control, yet curiously turned on. The stimulation was overwhelming, and I let out a whimper. I bit my lip, my fingertips gathering the bedding and squeezing it as his fingers pumped within me.

The feeling was like nothing I'd experienced before. As Hayes had told me it would, a wave of submission washed over me. My body and soul belonged to him. My pussy got wetter, my body relaxing. "Good girl. Your bottom responds so nicely to my touch." His fingers remained inside my ass as his other hand stroked my quivering bottom. "Daddy needs to punish you for not listening. Daddy's spankings aren't enough, are they, precious Luna? I need your full submission. And I'll get it by punishing this tight little bottom of yours."

I gasped as a sharp spank landed on my ass, leaving my cheek jiggling. He pressed his fingers further within me, causing my toes to curl and my legs to spread further. Another spank landed on the inside of my upper thigh. I cried out as the sting danced along my skin, his fingers pumping within my ass once more.

"Bad, bad girl. Let me feel that pussy and see if having Daddy play with your bottom makes you excited. I can smell it on you already." I panted as his free hand slapped my ass once more. Then, a finger from his other hand slipped inside my aching pussy. My ass was full, my pussy was full. My bottom was stinging from his spanks. My clit was pulsing, wanting nothing more than to be rubbed into an orgasm. "Just as I suspected—dripping wet. Naughty, naughty. My little girl loves when Daddy plugs her bottom. Time to punish this tight little hole with my cock."

"There's... there's no way it will... fit," I protested, looking over my shoulder at him. Nerves fluttered in my tummy while my nipples further tightened against the cool bedding.

"It'll fit." Slowly, he withdrew his fingers from me. My little stretched rosebud quivered as he made his exit. The inside of my bottom felt strangely empty, making me wonder what it would feel like when it was his big cock in my ass instead of his two fingers. My pussy wanted his fingers back inside me. I pressed my legs together, trying to give my aching clit some relief. A sweat broke out on my forehead; I was unsure of what would happen next.

His hand went to my waist, my skin tingling where he grasped me. My face burned with embarrassment as he guided me off his lap and stood me before him. My nipples were hard little pebbles, goosebumps rose on my chilled, nude skin as he looked over my body—the body his fingers had just entered in the most intrusive way. And that was nothing compared to what he had promised to do to me. Despite my fear, my pussy clenched, a gush of excitement pooling between my thighs.

My pussy tightened as he commanded, "Lie over the bed." Eager to be out of his all-consuming gaze, I turned around my back to him and quickly bent myself over the bed. Cool air rushed over my bare skin. My feet pressed into the carpet as I stretched my upper body, resting my face on my hands. Nerves danced in my stomach. My fingers trembled as they locked together beneath my cheek.

He left me alone, naked and lying over the bed, my bare ass fully exposed as I could hear him crossing the room. The familiar sound of the unzipping of a bag made me wonder, what could he possibly be retrieving? When I sensed he was once again behind me, I shuddered. Moisture pooled between my thighs as the sound of him unbuckling his belt filled the room.

"Spread those gorgeous legs," he demanded.

This was really happening. Hayes had complete control over me and I had no say in whether he would perform the dark act on my body. It scared me, and thrilled me, pushing me beyond my level of comfort into a zone of eroticism I had never experienced. Would it hurt? Would he even be able to get that massive cock inside my poor, tight little bottom? A sharp slap on my ass made me yelp and return to the moment.

I could hear the sound of my wetness as I spread my legs, obeying his command. Cold air rushed between my legs, caressing my folds and causing my pussy to tremble. The fronts of his thighs were against mine, his hard cock nestling in between my legs. I shifted my weight, spreading my legs further until I could feel the head of his cock pressed against the entrance of my pussy.

Surprised relief and a tinge of disappointment washed over me that he had not pursued my rosebud after all. He pushed his cock within me and I let out a great moan as he filled me. Slowly, his cock pressed further, my pussy responding with a tightening to every inch it was given. My sheath wrapped around him as a slow warmth traveled over my whole body. Pulling back, his fingers gripped into my hips as he thrust back in, hard and fast. I cried out in pleasure and pain as the full length of his cock pounded into my pussy. Shivers danced over my neck as one of his hands left my hip and gathered my hair into a knot, giving it a firm tug. I moaned as my head arched back.

My body was already so close to orgasm from lying over his lap, listening to his dirty words and having his fingers inside of my bottom. The submissiveness he had drawn from the center of my being remained heavy in my mind as his cock slammed me again and again.

My arousal heightened, my sheath tightening around him, milking him, squeezing his member. "I, I… I'm going to come," I gasped after only a few more of his intense thrusts.

"No, you're not."

My head snapped back toward him, my eyes widening. "Why not?"

"Bad girls don't get to come when they want. They come when they're told. And very bad girls come with Daddy's cock up their naughty little ass."

My mouth snapped shut, my face burying in my hands on the bed. Shame burned on my face. I was the good girl. Until Hayes I had had very nice, though mildly boring, missionary position sex. Maybe to mix it up once or twice, I wore something lacy to bed. The way Hayes spoke, the way he took ownership over my body, it had me melting in my core. A carnal desire for him to own me, to make me come, to have his cock in my ass, took over. I lay over the bed, legs spread, ready to take him.

His hand stroked my back, massaging my shoulders. "I'm going to lube up, then I'm going to take you in that pretty little ass." He spanked me twice, my teeth biting into my bottom lip as he did. There were a few soft noises, then,

I felt the tip of his lube-covered cock pressed against my rosebud. The jelly felt cold against my hot skin. Overwhelmed by sensation, tears sprang into my eyes as the head of his cock pushed into my unwilling entrance. My pucker quivered, not wanting to accept him. I took a deep breath, relaxing as he instructed, and breathed as he pushed the head of his cock past my tight, pulsing rim. With another deep breath, I welcomed the entire head of his member into my ass. His hands went to my hips, holding me possessively as he slowly guided his cock further within my bottom.

My skin stretched to capacity. The burning pain made way to a pleasurable fullness. The muscles of my ass wrapped tightly around him as he moved back and forth within me. His fingertips dug into my hipbones as he moaned, "Such a tight little ass. There's my good girl."

The submission I had felt from his fingers was nothing compared to what I felt as his entire cock buried itself within my ass. I moaned, tears leaving my eyes as he pulled out, then thrust back in.

His hand reached around my pelvis, his fingers finding my clit. I cried out as he plunged deeper within me from behind, his finger pressing into my engorged bud. I moved my hips, rubbing harder against his hand. Waves of pleasure pulsed through me as he circled my sensitive nub and fucked my ass. My toes curled into the carpet, my cries were high and shrill. My ass tightened hard, my pussy clenching as my body experienced ecstasy. White lights flashed behind the lids of my eyes as I came in a weeping, pulsing, shaking mess.

A few more thrusts and I could feel his cock pumping his hot seed into my ass. He came with a moan. He collapsed against my back, our damp skin pressing together. His lips caressed my ear as he whispered, "You're my entire world, Luna."

That night at the hotel, I lay on the bed, recovering from my day and the intense fucking session. I was overwhelmed with emotion from having anal sex for the first time. I couldn't believe how deeply I felt for Hayes and how the connection of our bodies further deepened the unbreakable bond between us.

Hayes and Brody went out to dinner, giving me a much-needed few hours to myself to decompress. Sometimes being grounded was a good thing.

I missed Little Peak.

I was too embarrassed to admit it to my friends, but New York just wasn't for me. I knew I should be enticed, energized by the sites, the people, the culture. I wasn't. I couldn't help it—I was just plain old Louanne Dixon, born in Little Peak and happy on the ranch. I missed my house, my bed, the Mess Hall. I kept my opinions to myself, happy the others were enjoying the trip. They had earned it.

Picking up the phone, I ordered room service for dinner. As I waited for the grilled chicken and champagne to arrive, I flipped through photos of chalkboard menu ideas, and a misspelled text came through on my phone.

*Memaw: Louanne I M texTING aren't you proud?*

*Me: Memaw, is this really you? Or is Colton doing the typing for you?*

*Memaw: Are you kidding itSaturday nightcolton is at Buds*

*Me: You are doing great, Memaw!*

*Memaw: THX I saw ur speech on the compter colton liverstreamed it for me sogood*

*Me: I'm glad you enjoyed it, Memaw 😊 and great job texting. I'll call you, now though. It will be easier.*

Smiling, I hit the call button. The phone rang four times before she picked up.

"Hello? Who is this?" she yelled into the phone.

"Memaw, it's Louanne. I just texted you that I was calling you," I said, holding back a laugh.

"Oh, hi, honey. I thought it was you. Just wanted to be sure it wasn't a telemarketer. You know how they love to call at this time of night. Right when you're sitting down to eat your supper."

"Nope. Just me, Memaw. Don't you have me programed into your contacts? My name should come up on your phone screen when I call," I said.

She gave a frustrated grunt. "I haven't figured out this dagnab contraption yet. I'm still hooked on my landline. You just punch the number in that you want to call. Easy as pie."

I held back an eye roll. I knew she could use easily use the cell phone Brody had bought her if she made any effort to. "I'll show you how to do it when I get home from New York. You can even put a picture of each person in so it will pop up when they call you."

"Now why on Earth would I need to see a picture of you all? I get to see the real thing nearly every single day when you are all sitting around the table telling me you're hungry," she joked.

I laughed, asking her, "How's it going there on the ranch?"

"It's going good." There was a pause. When she spoke again, I was surprised by her tone. It sounded as if she were nervous. "I wanted to let you know that I took that Pamela's advice."

"What advice was that?" I asked gently.

"I-I started my own cooking blog on the ranch's website," she said.

"You did? Good for you!" I said.

"I wrote down my bit and I had Colton make a webpage and type it up and everything. That was why I was texting you. To tell you great job on your speech. And that I want you to read my blog."

"That's so awesome. I'll be sure to check it out as soon as we hang up," I promised. I couldn't wait to read it.

She sighed. "I wanted to text you some of those Imogens too, but I couldn't get them to work."

"Memaw... what's an Imogens?" I asked, my brow furrowing as I tried to think of what she could possibly be talking about.

"You know… Imogens. The little pictures of poopie and such? I was going to send you a four-leaf clover for good luck on your speech, earlier," she said.

"Oh… *emojis*," I murmured.

"Imogens. That's what I said," she huffed.

I smiled. "Tell Colton to show you. It's easy once you get the hang of it."

"Will do, girly. Now get on to bed and don't let that cowboy fiancé of yours keep you up. You got another big day ahead of you tomorrow," she said.

"Okay, Memaw. I will."

"And Louanne—"

"Yes?"

Her voice was soft when she spoke. "We're all real proud of you, honey."

"Thanks, Memaw." After saying goodbye, I flicked through my 'Imogens,' sending her a pretty one of a red heart.

I took my iPad out of my purse, clicking it on and enjoying the blue glow that filled my room. Pulling up the CLAS website, I saw two new tabs. One marked Louanne's blog. The other marked Memaw's blog. Smiling, I pulled up Memaw's blog to read her first ever post.

*Memaw's Cooking Blog*

*Top Ten ways to not get carted off to a looney bin when cooking for a wedding*

I'm gonna do this like one of those countdowns they used to do on the music charts—you know, all the songs are great but the last one is the best one? Gosh, I sure miss sock hop and Motown music. Don't you? So much better than the trash they play on the radio these days. Though I do like that little Swift girl. She's a feisty one! Ok, so like I said, these are the Top Ten ways to not go crazy when you are preparing a meal for a wedding. They are going to go up in level of importance as your read the list.

*Note if you don't have all day to sit around on your butt reading because you have to cook for a wedding, just grab your wooden spoon and skip to number ten.

1.  Keep any and all opinionated women (apart from yourself) out of the kitchen. The last thing you need when cooking for a wedding is someone standing over your shoulder telling you how things ought to be done. If you have been charged with the job of cooking for one hundred people, do you really need someone telling you the 'right' way to grease a pan? I don't think so.

2.  Do not, I repeat, do not let the bride enter your kitchen. Food is ugly when it is being cooked and it doesn't look pretty till it hits the serving tray with the garnish. She does not need to see the process, only the final product. Have you ever seen a fish that still had its head attached to it? Those beady little eyes staring up at you? I rest my case.

3.  Make sure you communicate very clearly with your Louanne—whoever that may be. Though I pity you trying to cook for a wedding if you don't have yourself a Louanne as good as we do. She makes lists. Lots of lists. With little checkboxes on them so we don't forget anything. So, communicate. And make lists. Number three was a two for one. Lucky you.

4.  Don't burn the food. This one is self-explanatory but too important to not be mentioned.

5.  Don't undercook the food. Have you seen one hundred people with food poisoning? I haven't either but I'm imagining it right now while I'm writing this blog and it isn't pretty.

6.  Do not serve gaseous foods. The wedding party does not want to be out on the dance floor, shaking their junk, just to be rocket launched across the room by a booty explosion. Beans, beans, the magical fruit, the more you eat, the more you toot.

You get the picture? Some lesser known but highly powered foods to avoid are broccoli, cheese, and cabbage. (Side note: If you are planning on serving cabbage at a wedding, stop reading this blog and hit some cookbooks for new ideas.)

7. I second Louanne when she says to serve foods the bride and groom like. Let's be honest… that bride probably hasn't eaten in days, trying to fit into her perfect dress. And, now that she has that man on lockdown, she can gain all the weight she wants. Fill up her plate with all kinds of goodies and give her some energy for her wedding night. She's going to need it if you know what I mean. Wink, wink.

8. Don't lift all the heavy grocery bags yourself. You don't want to get a crick in your back and be laid up on the big day, having to holler instructions at your grandchildren from an armchair you had your grandsons drag into the kitchen. It isn't pretty.

9. Always cook more than you think you need. Do you really want hungry guests? I don't think so. Also, people go home sooner when they are chock full. That always works in the couple's favor because by the end of the night those two lovebirds are ready to get the heck out of there.

10. If you don't heed any of my other advice… heed this. The single most important way to keep your sanity when cooking for a wedding: Keep the men out of your kitchen. If you don't you will work all day and at the end of the day you will only have half the food to show for it. Those men pick and pick at the food till there is nothing left. Especially when you are frying bacon. Also, they are messy. You already have enough cleaning up to do at the end of the day. Hit them with your wooden spoon if you must. Just get them out of there.

Stay tuned for my next blog post… Mysterious stains on your kitchen linens; what they probably are and how to get rid of them.

I put down my iPad and picked up my phone. Finding my thread with Memaw, I typed in, "Best blog post ever, Memaw."

• • • • • • •

After ditching the conference the day before, I felt like I had to make up for lost time and attend every class possible. The day was a whirlwind of lectures. How to blog, how to get more blog followers, how to make more money on your blog, how to find new content for your blog. If I heard the word 'blog' one more time, I was going to lose it.

And then there were the adoring fans I didn't know I had. They circled me in between each and every class, demanding to know where I got my ideas, my décor, my food. How had all of these women heard about me, Louanne Dixon from Little Peak, Wyoming? They expected so much from me, their eyes gleaming with excitement, their voices strained with curiosity about what ideas I had for my own wedding.

The truth was… I did not have one single idea for my own wedding.

Returning to my hotel room, I collapsed onto the bed, only to find three emails from Eloise asking me for the details for my 'show-stopping,' big day for the article. Hayes came back from dinner to find me in a sobbing heap.

Gathering me into his arms and rubbing my back, Hayes asked, "Luna, what's wrong?"

"Hayes, I can't… I can't… I can't… marry you!" I wailed.

He froze, his arms stiffening. "What do you mean, sweetheart? You don't want to marry me?"

"Oh, no, Hayes! That's not it. I just mean, I can't possibly have a wedding!" I cried.

Hayes placed his hands on my cheeks, steadying me. His

gaze locked on mine, concern flashed in his eyes. "Louanne Dixon. Tell me what is going on."

I took a deep breath, pushing the sobs deep down into my chest. "It's too much pressure! From the magazine spread to the blog followers... they're all expecting this to be the end all, be all wedding that will put all other weddings to shame. And I just can't do it. I can't pull it off. Every time I try to look at flowers, or vases, or food platings, I break out in a cold sweat and get sick to my stomach. If I even hear the wedding march, I start to break out in hives. I-I love wedding planning for other people, but I can't plan my own wedding!"

He considered my face for a moment. Then, he murmured, "It's like the doctor who smokes, or the housekeeper who you find out is a hoarder. Or Mrs. Macklewitz."

My brow knit in confusion. "Mrs. Macklewitz? The sixth grade English teacher from Little Peak Middle? What does she have to do with this?"

Hayes said, "She couldn't spell. Remember? But she made you fall in love with the story. Taught you how to pick apart a book and delve into its every nook and cranny. Find foreshadowing hidden deep within the sentences. She was great at her job, but man, she was a bad speller."

I sniffled. "You're right. She was a great English teacher. And a terrible speller."

He stroked my hair in the most loving way as he spoke. "Does this have anything to do with your father not being there to walk you down the aisle?"

A cold chill ran through my body. My dad had left before the Jenkinses even moved to Little Peak. Hayes and I had never spoken about my father, or his leaving our family. "I-I suppose some of the... upset I'm feeling may be coming from that place. But I don't want to talk about it, Hayes. Ever."

"And we don't have to, Luna. I'm your daddy now. I'll take care of you till death us do part." He kissed the top of my head in the most endearing way. I melted under his caress, letting his words calm my mind. "You're under too much pressure, sweetheart. You say it yourself—planning a wedding can be the most stressful event of a young woman's life. And that's without all of the eyes of the world watching her, expecting to be wowed by her. It is too much. I hate to see you this unhappy, baby girl. Weddings are supposed to be happy." His mouth moved to the lobe of my ear, nibbling and biting. He whispered, "Let me make you happy again, baby girl."

I wiped the tears from my eyes with the backs of my hands. Hayes slid on top of me, pressing my back into the bed. I turned my head as his kisses trailed from my ear, down my neck. The tip of his tongue licked the tears from my skin. When he kissed my lips, I tasted the salt.

My mouth pressed against him as my body rose to meet his. My peaked nipples hardened against the muscles of his chest. My breasts felt heavy and longed to be freed from my bra. Hayes quickly unbuttoned my shirt, reaching his hand into the cup of my bra and squeezing my breast as he kissed and bit my neck. He murmured, "Let Daddy make it all better. Let all your stress go. Just feel everything Daddy is doing to celebrate your beautiful body."

I groaned, my eyes closing. His hand slipped up and into my skirt. "Such a beautiful woman. Such a good girl. I want to please you. I want to hear you sing for me." His hand grabbed my mound, squeezing. My aching clit longed for his attention. It did not have to wait long as Hayes disappeared underneath my skirts, murmuring, "Sing for me, baby," as he slipped my panties from my legs.

His tongue flicked between my slippery folds, finding my swollen, pulsing clit. As he licked and sucked, he slipped one, then two fingers inside of me. Cupping his palm around my bottom, he held me up in one hand, moving his fingers in and out, as his mouth continued to massage me. I forgot the stress of the day—I forgot everything. I focused on the sensation both inside and outside of my body as my hips rocked with pleasure. High, breathy noises escaped me as my sheath tightened around his fingers. My heels pressed into the bed. My hips stilled, my pelvis raised in the air, frozen as I waited for the delicious explosion to overtake me. I came in a burst of light and passion and sing for my daddy I did as a loud guttural scream left my chest. I shuddered, unable to move.

But he didn't stop. My knees were like jelly, my breath coming in pants. I begged. "Stop. I can't take it—" My words were cut off by whimpers and moans as his mouth brought me to a second orgasm. Tears stung my eyes as my insides constricted around his fingers once again. I came quietly, then collapsed onto the bed.

Hayes kissed his way up my body. He hovered over me. My fingertips outlined the muscles of his strong shoulders as he balanced his weight on his arms. His cock slid easily within my slick entrance, my pussy warm and welcoming and open to him. He thrust within me.

"Is baby happy again?" he asked.

Completely spent, I nodded. There wasn't an ounce of tension in my body. Every muscle felt relaxed as if I had just had a deep tissue massage. The orgasms had somehow cleansed me, purging me of unwanted thoughts. All that existed in my world was currently on the bed I lay on.

We rocked together as one. We came together as one. Afterwards, as we lay in each other's arms, our hair and skin damp from our lovemaking, I asked, "What do we do?"

"Do you still want to marry me?" he asked softly.

I smiled and said, "Of course. I just don't want to have a wedding."

His brow knit in thought as he asked, "Is it possible to have a marriage without a wedding?"

My fingertip traced lazy circles on his bare chest. "We could run away. Elope?" I suggested, though my heart wasn't in it.

Hayes shook his head, saying, "No. That would break the hearts of the people we love. They've waited for this nearly as long as we have." He was silent for a moment, then he said, "I think I have an idea."

• • • • • • •

Travel and Dining*'s CLAS Ranch Wedding Special*
*Best Wedding Ever, by Eloise Smarts*
*Always a wedding planner, never a bride.*

*That was the story of Louanne Dixon's life. Planning and preparing celebration after celebration but never participating. Watching each and every bride walk down the aisle on their perfect day—a day that she created for them—while never walking down the aisle herself.*

*Until last Sunday.*

*It was just another day in the quaint country church, Little Peak Baptist. Friends chatting on the front steps before the service. Emma and her sister Bessie fighting over who got the aisle seat. The reverend stumbling up to the altar just a minute behind schedule. But brows were raised in surprise when the first chords of the opening song were sung. Instead of 'I Need Thee Every Hour,' the church echoed with the words of the Blake Shelton tune, 'God Gave Me You,' sung by someone other than Little Peak's baritone, Brody Jenkins.*

*Brody, owner of CLAS ranch and brother of the groom, was too busy for singing. He was walking Louanne down the aisle. Hayes Jenkins appeared from the side door of the church. Standing proudly with love engraved on his face, he watched his bride gliding toward him in an elegant Vera Wang gown that looked as if it were designed with her in mind. Much to the surprise of Little Peak Baptist's congregations, Louanne and Hayes were wed on the altar of the darling country church.*

*When interviewed after the ceremony, groom Hayes shrugged and said, "All of our family and friends are in attendance on Sundays, so we figured, why not?"*

*Hayes' grandmother, Memaw was the only one in on the secret and spent the week prior to the wedding cooking and packing up a picnic to feed the one hundred churchgoers turned guests on the lawn of the church. Big red and white checked cloths were spread over the ground as basket after basket of food were unloaded. Fried chicken, potato salad, buttermilk biscuits, all homemade, were served.*

*For dessert, the bride herself walked around handing out individual portions of Hayes' famous homemade vanilla ice cream served in white ceramic mugs that proudly stated 'Jenkins Wedding Little Peak Baptist.' Guests were delighted to find an etching of the church at the bottom of their mugs. A parting gift to take home.*

*Devoted readers of Louanne's blog, and this magazine, had lofty expectations for America's Favorite Wedding Planner's wedding to be the best one ever.*

*And it was.*

*Because the best wedding ever is the one that you actually enjoy.*

*Cheers to Hayes and Louanne Jenkins.*

*Best of luck,*

*Eloise Smarts*

She was right. Wasn't that what it was all about? In a sea of tulle and cake and high heels, one should never lose sight of the purpose of the day. Two souls becoming one. Happily ever after.

Smiling, I put the magazine down on my bed. Looking out of the window, I sighed contentedly at the sight of the aquamarine waters. I had finally made it to my white sand beach on our Tahitian honeymoon. I could now cross it off my bucket list. I grabbed my phone, opening my notes app. The last list I had made stared back at me. I read it with a smile.

*Ten Things I Love About Being Married*

1. Honeymoons. Sun, sand, sex. Margaritas in glasses as big as my face. Getting spanked on the beach in my itty-bitty yellow polka dot bikini. Heaven.
2. Holding hands with my husband. His white-gold wedding band wrapped around his finger like a reminder of the promises we made one another.
3. Being called 'Mrs. Jenkins.' It doesn't make me feel old like I thought it would. It makes me feel like

'his.'

4.  Going to bed with my best friend every night.
5.  Waking up next to my best friend every morning.
6.  Married morning sex.
7.  I never have to make the coffee again. He's always up before me.
8.  I never have to drive again. He loves to drive. He even fills my car with gas.
9.  Being my daddy's little wifey.
10. Knowing that as long as we are alive, we will have one another's backs. Look out for one another. And love one another, forever.

As I scrolled down, my brow knit in confusion. Beneath my list was a new one—one I didn't remember writing. As I read it, my heart warmed, and tears sprang in my eyes. So that's why Hayes had demanded that as my husband he should be privy to my phone's passcode!

*Ten Things I Love About Louanne*

1.  She is my Luna, my moon goddess. I love to watch her sleep; her face is so beautiful in the moonlight, it hurts to look at.
2.  She is the most generous, giving woman I know. She invests everything she has in bringing others joy.
3.  Her creativity. She could throw a kick-ass party with not much more than whatever is lying around and her imagination.
4.  The way her sweet little ass jiggles when I spank it. And the fact that she is my naughty little girl who needs and wants to be spanked.
5.  The welling feeling I get in my chest when she calls me 'Daddy.' There is nothing in this world like it.
6.  The way her nose scrunches up when she laughs. It's beyond adorable.
7.  The way she looked at me when we said our vows.

I'll never, ever forget it.

8. The spirited girl she was when we first met. She's kept that spirit alive within her as she's grown into an amazing woman.
9. Her strength. Louanne has nerves of steel and is one of the hardest working people I've met.
10. She is my baby girl. And always will be.

I wiped tears from my eyes with the back of my hand. What had I done to deserve such a man? I was the luckiest wife in the world. And there was no list I could create that would ever bring someone more joy than I felt in that moment.

# EPILOGUE

*The List: A Wedding Planner's Complete Guide to avoiding catastrophes and creating miracles*

By: Louanne Jenkins

A forward to my dear readers:

If marriage is the fabric of society, then weddings are the weaving of the fabric. And lists are the stitches that put the two together. Over the past decade I have planned and coordinated over one hundred weddings. Some, I cried tears of frustration over. Some, tears of joy. Each and every one different from the last. No two weddings are the same. No two brides are the same. And for each and every one of those brides and weddings, there have been lists.

Lists are what keep a wedding planner sane. Lists are what give a bride a center of peace during what is to be one of the most hectic times of her life. Lists offer insurance that nothing will be forgotten.

And at the end of the day, is there anything more satisfying that placing a checkmark inside a tiny box, signifying a job well done?

And every box checked signals a bride taking one more step toward that gorgeous rose petal-dotted aisle.

Under the suggestion of my husband, I have complied

all of those lists for you, and created a book. Use it as a roadmap to begin your journey into wedding planning. Or, have a cup of tea, browse its pages, and get a glimpse into the life of a wedding planner, through her many lists.

Happy Reading,
Louanne Jenkins

Publishers note: *The List: A Wedding Planner's Complete Guide to avoiding catastrophes and creating miracles* by author Louanne Jenkins eventually made it to the *New York Times* Bestseller list. When interviewed about the achievement, Louanne said she was stunned, humbled, and honored. When asked how it felt for a woman who loved making lists to have her name on one of the most important lists in America, Louanne confused the readers by stating, "Second most important, actually. The first most important list my name is on is hidden away in the notes app of my phone."

# THE END